From the author of  *ISLAND IN THE LAKE,*
and ISLAND IN THE LAKE,
an extraordinary new adventure . . .

TOWERS OF THE EARTH

ISH-O-TOBI

A lost starveling among a new tribe. As one of
the last hopes to carry on the tradition of the
Geh-i-nah, he was taken under their wing. And
taken to heart by the woman who gave him that
chance . . .

AYINA

The wise prophet, the ruthless hunter, and mysterious mistress of the healing arts. She fought
for her people, for their spirit, for their strength,
for their very survival in a strange new land. To
the Geh-i-nah she was their history, and their
future . . .

Praise for Ardath Mayhar's
PEOPLE OF THE MESA:

"Ardath Mayhar takes a bold look at the
mysterious Anasazi . . . Her characters are
living, breathing men and women who laugh,
cry, love and marry, share jokes and sadness.
Equally well described is their homeland,
harsh yet beautiful, demanding but rewarding.
May we see more of Ardath Mayhar's Anasazi,
the ancient ones of the Mesa."

—**Don Coldsmith, author**
of *The Spanish Bit Saga* and *The Changing Wind*

Diamond Books by Ardath Mayhar

PEOPLE OF THE MESA
ISLAND IN THE LAKE
TOWERS OF THE EARTH

TOWERS
O F · T H E
EARTH

ARDATH MAYHAR

DIAMOND BOOKS, NEW YORK

This book is a Diamond original edition,
and has never been previously published.

TOWERS OF THE EARTH

A Diamond Book/published by arrangement with
the author

PRINTING HISTORY
Diamond edition/February 1994

ISBN: 1-55773-980-3

Diamond Books are published by The Berkley Publishing Group,
200 Madison Avenue, New York, NY 10016.
DIAMOND and the "D" design
are trademarks belonging to Charter Communications, Inc.

PRINTED IN THE UNITED STATES OF AMERICA

10 9 8 7 6 5 4 3 2 1

To my husband, who though still recovering from cancer treatment, drove all the way as I traveled through the terrain that is the context of this book. Videotaping, making notes, absorbing the countryside, and driving cannot be done simultaneously.

PREFACE

As with all novels set in prehistory, this is a work of the imagination. Yet it is set in a real area of what is presently New Mexico, and it uses, as much as possible, the existing ruins and artifacts that have been found in the place I use as the setting of the stone houses.

It is my method to place real people (whose minds were as highly developed as ours) in real places, dealing with the problems that existed, according to archaeologists, ethnologists, and meteorologists, then and there. This story takes place some time during the thirteenth century, at which time the cliff dwellers on Mesa Verde were also at the peak of their culture.

My husband and I visited New Mexico on two different occasions, the first of which provided the mountainside setting of Ayina's refuge at the time the story begins. In the summer of 1992, we traveled west of that area, near the Chama River and along the roads that bracket the Gallina River.

Local people directed us to the tiny roads leading up Gallina Peak, which stands over the forested river canyon. A native of the area also gave detailed descriptions of the stone houses, in which he had played as a child.

He directed us to one of the ruins that is still standing, but because of the size of our van and the condition of the road we did not make it all the way there, to my regret. But older people with health problems don't take chances of being stranded in the wilderness, miles from any help.

We did travel along the ridge overlooking the river, walk among the trees, which, though cut over for timber, are still impressive, and look down into that canyon up which Ayina's people came to the sites where they built their homes. Knowing the kinds of trees, animals, birds, and insects, not to mention the smell of the air, helps in recreating the past.

It is, of course, impossible to assert that the people whom I call the Geh-i-nah came from the eastern part of this country. However, people who, over a long period of time, traveled from Asia to the Americas and spread their presence even to the tip of South America, surely were readily mobile.

The pottery found in the Gallina-Largo digs in this area is often pointed at the bottom, like the pottery found among the eastern tribes. There could easily have been a plague of some type, perhaps even brought by early Scandinavian travelers to the Atlantic coast, that would drive people from their longtime homelands.

The wonderful thing about fiction is that you can *pretend* that these things happened. Then you can introduce your people, put them into the places where they existed, face them with the problems they must surmount, and send them out to deal with the things you can find that may well have obtained at that time.

I have not tried to provide them with recognizable AmerIndian cultural background. As time passes, languages, religions, myths alter, and what these lost people believed, what rituals they used or gods they worshiped may still live as ghosts in present-day cultures. Too many changes have occurred, many of them instigated by a past government policy of destroying the Indian cultures and religions. One might as well create a Church of England priest in the time of Henry VIII by studying a modern Episcopal minister.

In any event, this is not history. This is a fantasy, created around a lost culture, a lost people, a lost time. As such it was a joy to write, and I hope that it will be a pleasure to read.

Ardath Mayhar
Nacogdoches, Texas
January 1993

TOWERS OF THE EARTH

➷1➶

The plaintive notes of a bone flute wavered along the constant breeze that blew across the mountain. The pines whispered, their resinous scent mingling with the odors of multitudes of green plants that grew in this high country at the head of a river.

Ayina sorted through the mesh bag of fragrant leaves she had gathered for cooking and making medicines, but she was aware of the freshness of the day. She raised her head and stared at the sky, where a hawk braced himself on the wind and circled high.

Before the season turned, she would be alone in her rude lodge. Only four old men, of all her Geh-i-nah people, would remain in the small cluster of shelters they had built on this height to which they had fled from the stone houses of their clans. Those had been built on promontories that thrust out over the canyon holding that other river. The people there had been wise and powerful, building so as to command every approach to their homes.

1

The thought of returning there both intrigued and chilled her. Never in all her long tale of days had Ayina been other than busy and useful, called in many directions at once to birthing women or children with broken bones or men desperately injured while hunting or in battle.

Even here, with so few left to attend, she was constantly occupied. *Not to be needed* . . . that was a concept so alien to her mind that her busy fingers stopped sorting the herbs as she thought about it.

Even as a child she had been learning the healing arts, as well as weapons and hunting and war. Each individual of the Geh-i-nah, however young or old, had to be capable of doing any task necessary at any time, given the need. In the dangers that surrounded her people, both killing and healing had been valued skills.

Because great healers existed among them, when her natural abilities became obvious she had been sent to Susuni, the old healer, for training. She could only hope that she was teaching her granddaughters as well as she had been taught.

She was fortunate, she knew, to have been granted the rearing of these three young women, who were about to leave her for new homes. They could so easily have died with the rest of the families who sheltered on the heights, instead of being hidden away by Ayina's own sister.

As they grew, often even Ayina's arts had been tested to the utmost in keeping them alive when fever had shaken their childish bones. Now they were going to strong young husbands and to clans that would value their skills, which were great.

Teala was perhaps the most intuitive of the girls, able to sniff a sufferer's skin, taste a fingertip dipped in urine, or simply watch the color of her patients. If Teala had been her own grandchild, the young woman couldn't have been more a born healer. Netah and Pulap were dutiful and skilled, but both lacked the instinctive feel for diagnosis their kinswoman showed.

Ayina wondered if her granddaughters would have proved even more skilled, if they had lived. But that thought roused bitter memories that she pushed from her consciousness. She had saved these children, but her own had died as the house of their people burned before her eyes. The child's cry that had come to Ayina's ears had haunted her dreams in the many seasons since.

She rose from her seat on a broad split of rock and folded the bag of leaves flat. All too soon the young men from the north and west would travel to the crooked peak, where they would meet the Geh-i-nah bringing their new wives.

The girls must be ready, their leather aprons and cloaks stitched with colored quills, their sandals woven into beautiful patterns, their cloaks of dressed deer hide and fur as attractive as it was possible to make them. When the time came to travel westward, all would be in order.

Already, their minds were filled with much of the lore Ayina could give them. The Ahye-tum-datsehe were fortunate in gaining these new wise women to be healers in their clans on their high mesas.

She trudged down the path between leaning bushes and pungent pines, her basket of herbs and roots bumping against her thin legs. The song of the flute grew louder, joining the pipings of unseen birds as she pushed through the thick growth and approached the lodge she shared with the young women. Those, if not granddaughters of her flesh, were granddaughters of her spirit.

Old Abani must be sitting behind the group of shelters, keeping his restless fingers busy on the holes of the flute as he dedicated his scanty breath to his pipings. Lacking any need in this tiny group for arrows and shaft straighteners and other tools, his friend Pahket made other things, from clay pipes to bone beads, and Ayina was glad he had made the new flute. Arthritic Abani needed something to take his mind from his affliction.

A burst of laughter sounded from beyond Ayina's lodge, and she set the baskets aside and went around to the clump of trees that sheltered the hut on the downhill side. Teala swayed in the tiny clearing, to the music of Abani's flute.

Pulap drummed softly on a hoop over which a bit of deer hide had been stretched, her rhythms soft and subtle. Netah circled, her feet stamping puffs of dust from the ground as she and Teala danced to the rhythm of the drum.

Sekto and Eketan, pretending to doze, their wrinkled eyelids all but closed, were watching and listening to the celebration as they leaned against the back of the third lodge, their flea-infested yellow dogs nestled close to their robed legs. Ayina knew that they, too, felt a sense of impending loss.

She paused to watch. Her smile was touched with sadness, for there would be few such playtimes left to her borrowed family. When the girls left for their new homes, the old men would sink into lassitude, and she herself might lose the will to live. She had seen such things happen often in the many hands of seasons that were her life.

Without disturbing the music and the dancing, she retreated to the lodge and hung the herbs to dry. Once she had arranged her loot satisfactorily, Ayina went outside again to check the pot sitting close beside the cook fire on its pad of flat stones from the river. Hot oblongs of rock lay among the red coals, and she lifted one between wooden tongs and dumped it into the waiting stew of young dog, venison, wild turnip, and fragrant leaves.

It had not cooled too much. One of the girls must have been keeping watch on the single meal of their day. Ayina squatted beside the fire, stirring the food with a peeled stick, thrusting dry branches into the fire when it burned low. The scent was savory, and she knew that the others would soon come to join her.

As she fanned the smoke from her face, she felt a pang of loss. When the girls went, she would lose her reason for living. And when *she* was gone, all the long history of her people and theirs would drift away on the wind like the smoke of this fire. The old men were already losing the threads winding among their ancient memories.

She had told the tales when her charges were small, sitting in the lodge while the wind shrieked around the curve of poles and hides covering their shelter. Their round black eyes had reflected the dangers and the labors told in that long story, as she took them back along the line of storytellers who had passed down the history of the Geh-i-nah.

It would be a long while, yet, before the bride-grooms arrived at the meeting place. She must tell the tales again, making certain that they would be remembered and told yet again to the children of these young ones. Even though her granddaughters were going to a new people with a different history, they must not forget their own.

The flute wavered and the drum thudded like a quiet heart. She could see, behind her eyelids, the dancing girls, the piping elder, the old men pretending to sleep, though their withered loins ached for youth again. She wondered if she could bear to be isolated here with them, once the young ones were gone.

A puppy yipped shrilly, and she threw him a bone fished from the stew. Sitting on her haunches, dreaming into the flames, she remembered her own youth, when she had danced among the maidens, circling the fire as their mothers watched and the young men sat in the shadows, admiring their beauty.

In the shadow of the forest, the stone houses bulked dark beneath a sky that was filled with drifts of stars. Flutes and drums made music that drove her young feet faster and faster, as the arm-linked girls moved, 'round and 'round. Keeping her eyes down, smiling softly, she thought of Nosete, somewhere out there in the dimness beyond the mountains and the desert. He was thinking about her, she knew, though he had not spoken to her on his family's last visit to her people.

She knew that, and her mother also knew, though they had said nothing about the matter. In time, the western Geh-i-nah would visit here with gifts and long talk, as they arranged for the marriage of their children.

She jerked awake and opened her eyes. She, too, was getting old and apt to fall asleep without warning. But she was not ready for that. She was unwilling to loose her grip on life as yet, for she felt a need in her bones to travel yet again, once her young ones were settled.

She cocked her head and heard the piping end, the drum thud to a soft climax. They would come soon. It would please her granddaughters to hear the old tales again, when the late-spring storms swept the high country and penned them into the lodges.

Smiling, Ayina pulled the pot away from the fire pad and lined up hollowed gourd bowls neatly beside it. Steps sounded close by, and the bright-eyed girls pushed into the cleared space about the cook fire, laughing about those secrets that so amused the young. Behind them, Abani leaned on Pahket's arm, while Sekto and Eketan followed their fellows eagerly toward the scent of food.

Ayina raised her head and stared upward beyond the treetops. Dark cloud was sailing down from the heights to the west and north. Even the weather was her friend, it seemed.

"Come and eat," she said to the seven who were all of her people. "And then, if it rains or snows, I shall tell you stories about our people."

It would snow, she knew, for she recognized that sharp scent on the wind that was still balmy with spring. Here on the shoulders of the mountains, even in summer there was often snow; as she scraped her gourd bowl clean with the wooden spoon Pahket had carved, she waited for the cloud to arrive.

And when the snow began, she took a brand from the outdoor fire into the lodge and kindled the wood in the fire pit. Teala fastened the door-flap, and the long tale of the Geh-i-nah began.

⋉2⋊

"So it was told to me by my mother's father, who had it from his own father's grandfather. In the days before the great journey, our people lived far, far to the east, across many rivers of water that drowned the unwary, in country that was forested and low and wet. These were the words of Zuasi, who was very old when I was a child," Ayina began. "Hear her tale from my lips:

"We lived there for many lives of men, and our crops were rich when we planted beans or squash, though wild plants grew so abundantly near the waters and in the forest that this was seldom done. The streams were busy with fat fish, and we wove nets of reed fiber and caught them in great numbers. Indeed, so rich was that country that I have wondered why a people so blessed with food would leave it.

"Yet the tale my ancestors told was one of sickness that came with a spring, when the first trading people visited the village; it did not leave again. The Anensi

9

arrived with the harvest of the cattail shoots, and they were racked with fever and covered with rashes when they came. This is the thing that happened. . . ."

Elipitu had been the principal leader of his people for five winters, and they were well pleased with him. The seasons had been mild, summers not too heavy with heat, winters not too snowy. The food-plants in the streams and the glades had offered great stores of stuff to keep for the cold season, and even after the winter past there was still a little fat to be found on a few of those now stirring their bones for the spring tasks awaiting them.

He felt a bit smug, for he was certain that it was his meticulous observance of the rituals, his constant watch on conditions in forest and water, his care for his families in the village that had much to do with this. When the first of the Anensi was spotted by the youngster assigned to watch the trails from the highest of the nearby trees, Elipitu was pleased.

His people made sturdy baskets from the reeds in their streams. They formed useful pots with pointed bottoms that could be steadied in the soft dirt beside the cook fires. The Anensi were always glad to trade salt, copper, and flint for the handwork of the Geh-i-nah. The strange beasts they brought were welcome, as well, providing amusement for children and adults alike.

When young Oket whistled the call of a jay, the chief rose from his shady spot beside his third wife Solata, who was expecting their second child at any moment, and went out to meet the newcomers. Not every year saw a visit from the traders, and it had been too long since he had met with Afe-yo, the long-time chief of the Anensi.

The group that came into sight along the path by the stream was smaller than usual. As Elipitu watched them come, he realized that there were no children among them and few of the very old. His heart chilled as he saw Afe-yo stride forward, his face hidden by his deer-hide robe, his hand raised to warn away the approaching children.

"We have sickness with us, brothers of the Geh-i-nah," the man called. "Do not come near, for it seems that it jumps from one man to the next, from child to mother to grandfather. We have lost a third of our number in the past four moons."

Elipitu had never faced a problem of this sort. Storms and droughts, floods and the failure of food sources were things that everyone knew, sooner or later. There were a few enemy peoples who warred with his own kind over fishing spots or rich hunting grounds, and he had known battle since becoming leader.

Sickness was something that filled him with dread, for it came silently and without warning. Yet he knew the Anensi well. It was their visits for trade, sometimes once in three or four summers, that supplied the things that his people could not make for themselves. They were not only allies but friends of all they knew, and he was unwilling to turn them away from his village.

"I will not ask to camp among you," Afe-yo called. "But we would like to stop here to rest and hunt and trade for grain and other foodstuffs. We have not had the strength to provide for ourselves since we crossed the Great Water, a moon past."

"I will talk with the elders and the women," Elipitu replied. "We will supply food and wood for your fires, for I can see that you need to break your journey here. Find a place to your liking, while I consult with my people. The young men will bring baskets of vegetables, for our gardens are rich and we have more than we can use or dry for winter."

. He surveyed the sorry string of travelers, feeling a surge of shock and pity. These were surely not the Anensi he knew, tall and erect, filled with pride and achievement as they went from tribe to tribe, supplying needed items and taking away unneeded ones. These were thin, worn, wretched people, the women scarred with the ritual cuts of grief, the men grim and on the point of dropping where they stood.

As Elipitu turned, Afe-yo lowered his robe, and the leader stopped and turned to look again at his old friend. The long, intelligent face was spotted red with rash, the skin drawn tightly over the bones, the eyes rheumy and filled with fever.

With a shudder, the Geh-i-nah leader turned again and hurried away to the village and his people. Surely they must give a place to rest to these tormented people, but he felt deep in his heart a cold certainty that his own people were now at risk.

Solata had risen and was making her awkward way toward the distant shapes of the newcomers, but he motioned for her to stop. "There is danger there," he told her. "I beg you—do not go among the Anensi on this visit. They are sick, and the child you carry might be harmed. Ill spirits live among them, jumping from one to the next, Afe-yo told me. I would not have any of my own kind go near enough for one to jump upon him."

She looked up, her dark eyes wide and disturbed. "The children . . . ," she murmured. "They will want to see these strangers!" She turned, her loosely draped garment of deer hide swirling, and hurried with heavy steps toward the place in the edge of the forest where the smallest children played, pretending to hunt or fish or wage war.

She would give the warning, Elipitu knew, and all the mothers would watch their small ones in order to keep them safe. He would not have to worry about the very young. It was those older children—the boys who were almost men and the girls who were not quite women—who gave him pause. They were filled with energy, alive with questions, curious as raccoons.

How could he keep them from going too near to that demon-ridden camp and bringing back the sickness to his village? He worried about that as he reached the center of the village and called out the wise old men and women to come and talk.

Zoheki hobbled from the shade of the forest, where he had been carving wooden bowls and spoons. Tabban rose from among the women who were stripping reeds to make fiber for baskets. Old Ertibbe, mixing pot clay in the shadow of her lodge, hauled herself upright by catching onto a passing boy, who obligingly stood still as she used her arms to raise the weight that her old legs no longer could manage to bring upright.

Daran and Feneto, together as usual, brought with them the nets they were weaving as they answered Elipitu's call. In a short while the five of them huddled in a circle beside Elipitu's house, listening with growing alarm to his words.

When he was done, they looked about them, and he knew they were reading the expressions and even, perhaps, the thoughts of these people they had known for so long. When Zoheki opened his mouth to speak, Elipitu knew what his words would be, even before he said them.

"We cannot turn away our old friends. But we cannot allow our people to go near them, either. We will supply food. We will send out the young men to hunt—the boys can go, too, for that will keep them busy and also away from that other camp. We will make them fresh sandals and loincloths, for they probably need those things. But there will be no sitting together around the mosquito fires at night, listening to long tales."

Zoheki paused and looked into Elipitu's eyes. "I fear, with you, that the young may infest themselves with the demons the Anensi bring with them. I fear, but what can we do, other than the thing I propose?"

There was a murmur of agreement from the small circle of elders. Tabban swatted her hands against her bare thighs and grunted, "Children are so fearless! How can we make them see the danger?"

But she knew, as they all knew, that only the old see danger. The young see only interest and opportunity, and only when the snake bites, the cougar springs, the rock falls will they believe in the possibility of their own deaths.

Honor must be served, Elipitu knew. Indeed, not one of the Geh-i-nah did not grieve for the Anensi, who continued to sicken, even as they remained in their camp, fed by their neighbors and given herb remedies by Ertibbe's daughter, Kelita, the healer of her people.

Plantain poultices seemed to ease the fire of the rashes, and all the children old enough to gather plants were sent to bring baskets filled with the long green leaves and pale roots. Yet Kelita said that she could see, even from a distance, that the sick did not get better but only shivered and moaned and died.

The summer passed in the usual sequence of labors, gathering food for the winter, drying meat and seeds and vegetables against the cold wet weather. But always there was that distant glimmer of fires, and occasionally there came the doleful chant as one of the Anensi died and was burned, as was the custom of that wandering people. Never was the feel of death absent from Elipitu's heart, and he grieved as if his own brother had died when Afe-yo's woman signaled to him, across the distance between, that her man had gone into the flames.

The sight of those death fires subdued even the children. Even those youths who had been most curious about the Anensi stopped asking questions and grew silent and cautious.

Summer waned, and the sickness had carried away half those Anensi who had come to the Geh-i-nah village. When the first cool wind came down from the north, the new leader, a very young man called Ro-ni, set his people to work gathering everything they possessed and packing it for travel. Still keeping his distance, he came to the invisible line the two tribes had agreed upon and called to Elipitu.

"We go now. Those who are going to die have done so. Those who have lived through the sickness are gaining strength and can now travel. We have much gratitude for the kindness of your people, and we hope, one day, to return, laden with useful goods, and trade with you as we used to." The words were brave and mature, but the young voice cracked with emotion as the boy turned and led his people away down the stream, toward the next long-delayed stop on their wide circuit.

Two days passed. The children rummaged about where the camp had been, picking up stray bits and pieces of rubbish that had not been worth taking away. A double hand of days after that the first child sickened.

"The demons stayed behind when the Anensi went," Ertibbe mourned, tears guttering down the deep wrinkles of her cheeks.

Elipitu felt tears inside himself, but he was chief and must not allow them to show. Instead he turned to Kelita. "How sick is small Gani? Does she have the red spots on her skin?"

Kelita nodded. "I have poulticed them with cool mud and plantain and the mixture of nettle and elder blossoms steeped together. The itching eases, but the fever is not made better, even with willow bark tea. She burns and cries, and I fear that I cannot save her. Gani is too small and too sick to survive an illness like this."

It was true. And when Gani had been put in her small pit and a mound of rocks piled upon it, another child sickened. Then another and another, until Elipitu came to a terrible decision.

Gathering the elders once more, he said, "We must go, as the Anensi did, trying to leave behind those demons that have camped where the traders stayed. Kelita has agreed to remain here and care for the small ones, and the mother of Telippi refuses to leave him. Ertibbe says that she is too old to leave this place that has always been the permanent village of our people, and she will also remain here."

There was a mutter of protest, but he held up his hand. "You saw that the Anensi had no children among them. Not a single one, except those living, unborn, in the bellies of their mothers. Are you willing to risk our small ones?"

Tabban looked about at the old men. "Of course not!" she spat. "And even these old fools know that much. We will go. I will be at the heels of the young people, never fear, and we will move with tomorrow's dawn."

The leader sighed with relief. With that fierce old woman driving them, his people would uproot themselves and move quickly, leaving behind, he devoutly hoped, the sickness that was creeping among the children of the Geh-i-nah.

Ayina sighed, coming slowly back to the present, and looked about at her listeners. "At that point, old Zuasi said, 'But they did not leave behind that sickness in one move or in two. Over the next hand of winters they moved twice more, and then again. West they went, toward the setting sun, and after a long time they came to the edge of the forests and looked out over land that lay flat and treeless as far as they could see.

" 'It was frightening to leave the shelter of the trees,

the frequent streams of good water, and the foods
they knew. Still, Elipitu drove them forward, and the
memory of those they had left behind in grave pits
helped him to keep them in motion, as year followed
year and the demons, growing less powerful now, still
stalked them.

" 'When they were at last free of those demons, they
were in the midst of a land so harsh that there was
no question of remaining there as a permanent home.
Surely, Elipitu thought, there must be forests beyond
these endless plains, waters that flowed abundantly,
and a place in which his homeless people might live
again, rooted and stable.

" 'But it was very long, and other leaders than he
lived and died before they came to such a place.'
That was the tale of Zuasi, who was old when I was
young." And again Ayina glanced about at her granddaughters and the old men who had crowded into her
house to hear that long-familiar tale from her lips.

⋊3⋉

The child stumbled along blindly. He was exhausted, hungry, bruised, and terrified in almost equal parts, though he never paused for more than long enough to catch his breath. When he did halt, he took cover in thickets or behind one of the rocky shoulders that thrust at intervals from the mountainside.

At such times he listened, his small head cocked, his eyes closed to intensify his hearing. He could hear birds beginning their mating calls, branches, now budding or newly leafed, stirring in the breeze that swept the mountain. He could hear the distant rush of water in the river below the slope he was climbing.

The voices of the men were silent. It would have been better, he thought, if they had shouted or called after him. They might have seemed more human. As it was, they hunted him with the same noiseless intensity he had seen in the hunting habits of the puma and the lynx.

He shivered and started off again, going up at a long slant toward the shaggy crest of the ridge that edged the river. His short legs ached with effort, and he knew that it *would not be long before he could run no longer. Then they would catch him and take him back to their village. What might happen then did not bear thinking about.*

The mountainside curved, and he found himself facing a bastion of stony outcrops that pushed out over the canyon below. Good cover, though that would be the first thing his pursuers would search, he knew. Still . . . he might be able to see a long way from the lip of that rocky cliff.

He lay flat and snaked along, ignoring the scratches as sharp edges cut his skinny belly and knees and elbows. Sliding between chunks of splintered stone, he made his way forward until he could see far down the river canyon, where the new green of spring made the forest look misty.

He shaded his eyes against the morning sun. Was that a hint of movement, far down the canyon? He lay flatter, peering from behind an angle of rock. Yes. Someone moved on the game trail that edged the water. One finger count . . . two . . . three . . .

He did not wait to finger-count any more who might come. He had to change his route, to throw the hunters off his track.

He found, beyond the prow of the great cliff, a smooth face of stone that slanted into the river itself. It was a long way down; he knew he might be killed if he risked that descent, but he had to cross the river without leaving any track to show those dreadful men where he had gone.

Gulping his tears, the boy launched himself down the rockface. He rolled, tumbled end over end, bumped and scraped his way, amid a rattle of gravels and larger stones, to the bottom, where he splashed into the cold water and went under.

Desperately, he pushed down with both hands and feet and shot to the surface. As soon as he cleared his nose, he stared downstream, fearful that his pursuers might have heard the splash. But there was no movement, no sound except water against rocks.

They were too far away. He had barely located them from the height above, and they were following the lower route, which curved around toes of woods and rocks extending into the stream. He felt for the bottom with his feet, finding a boulder on which to brace himself, for the moment, against being swept downstream.

Like most of his people, he had never learned to swim, but he had to cross the river, no matter what happened. Drowning could not be worse than what waited for him in the village down there in the lowlands, he thought. Kicking off from the boulder, he shot forward, the current turning him over and over.

He flailed desperately with both arms, kicked his feet, and somehow he found himself in an eddy behind a lump of rock on the other side of the stream. He caught a rough knob with both hands and hauled himself along beside the stone, where the rock was already wet with splashing waves.

He lay there, panting, snorting water, comforting his chilled body against the sun-warmed stone. When he had stopped shivering too hard to stand, he rose and moved, stooping, behind the shelter of the outcrop, heading up the pebbly slope toward a fringe of young trees and thick bushes higher on the mountainside.

They would not expect him to be across the water. They did not swim, any more than his own kind did, he was sure. It would seem impossible that anyone as small and frail as he could make it through the turbulent river, swollen with spring runoff and icy as the snow itself. When they did not find any trace over there, they might well try to cross themselves, but by then he intended to be far from the river, *hidden in some cranny that might save his life.*

He might starve. Some beast might eat him. He might freeze in the night or fall and break his neck, but he would not return to the lowlands and the fate those men and their priests intended for him. He had heard their talk, in the night before he escaped. He understood more than they thought. He did not intend to die for the gods of those alien men who had stolen him from his own kind.

The fitful spring weather had turned very warm. Teala sat before the lodge, forming a basket with quick, skillful fingers, while Pulap sorted freshly picked leaves of medicinal plants into their assorted piles. Ayina, watching, thought how beautiful they were, how wise for their years.

Perhaps living so alone, so separate from any other kind of people, had made the girls think more deeply than was usual for the young. A small group being particularly vulnerable, Ayina had avoided the notice of any hunters or gatherers coming into the heights from among the people who lived in the valleys below. She had known the work of enemies to her great cost, and she had no intention of risking this tiny remnant of the Geh-i-nah to the mercies of some tribe about which she knew nothing.

For a time, she moved between her tasks inside the hut and the girls before the door. Then, finishing her indoor work, Ayina gathered up the deerskin robe she was decorating for Pulap and went outside to sit beside the two girls while they waited for Netah to bring fresh supplies of herbs from the patch up the steep slope above their village.

"Sekto went with Netah," said Teala, who was

weaving the reed segments into an interesting pattern without thinking about what her fingers were doing. "I think he is beginning to realize that the granddaughters are about to leave. His mind seems to have become as dim as his eyesight."

Ayina said nothing, but she agreed with Teala. The ancient man had been told of the offer for the young women, and he had grinned his toothless smile. Yet there had been little comprehension in his milky gaze, though she knew that he had possessed a very sharp mind until recently. As she had told the old tales, he had listened with more attention than before, and at last he seemed to recognize the fact that soon he would be alone with Ayina and his equally old and decrepit companions.

She felt for him, knowing that his was the sweetest disposition among the old men under her care. Pahket was skilled, quick of wit, sharp of eye, but always ready to make trouble if he could. Abani was very wise, very kind, but he was so crippled now, his hands twisted almost past tending himself, that he spoke little. Eketan, who was the brother of her mother, had not only gone lame but had withdrawn into that other world where the very old often go to escape the reality of their infirmities.

No, only his eyes limited Sekto, when he chose to pay attention to the world around him. She would have liked to discuss the future with him, but she knew that he would not like to talk about that. His future held only death. And though none of her people had ever feared the end of life, she had learned with amusement that the very old seemed to cling tightly to what was left.

Her own future, by contrast, held a great unknown span of time, for she was much younger than the men. Would she—*could* she—remain here on this mountainside to tend these oldsters? That seemed a waste to her orderly mind.

Still, she could not go with her granddaughters to their new home, that was clear, for new people had different ways. It was unwise to put into a new tribe an old woman who knew that the rules and rituals imposed by leaders, whatever their kind, are only empty gestures raised against things that can neither be known nor controlled.

Ayina set a dyed quill into place and secured it tightly against its neighbor. The girls murmured between themselves, but she withdrew into her own thoughts. She lived there, now, more than in the world of the mountain or her lodge or even that of her companions.

Becoming older was in some ways limiting, as bones and muscles wore and ached, but in others it was liberating. She understood things now that had thwarted and angered her when she was young. She had wondered rebelliously why there must be rules for conduct that the very young must observe. That had troubled her when she stood at the door-flap of life.

Now she understood that such seemingly harsh strictures were the only protection the young possessed against the terrible and unguessable dangers of living. She had guided her granddaughters with just such rules, altered to suit their very different circumstances. There were perils beneath every step, in every tree, beyond every rock, and the young did not understand that.

She sighed and set another quill into place. She also understood that those attempts at safeguarding her people were all but useless. The teachings of those who had trained her seemed unreasonable, when she was the age of Teala. Now she understood the desperate need that had formed them and the aching concern of those who taught them.

Nothing meant what it seemed to mean, and that was a bitter lesson to learn as one aged.

She raised her head, listening. Steps, quiet and yet audible to one whose life had hung upon her detection of approaching feet, whispered on the mountainside. "They are coming," she said, her fingers busy with the quills and the deer hide.

In a bit, Netah came down the path, holding on to Sekto's arm to keep his uncertain steps from wandering from the solid rock and soil onto the dangerous edge of the slope. She held a basket overflowing with leaves and stalks and roots, a rich early harvest that promised well for the summer to come.

Pulap rose to help her get the old man safely onto the flat space where their small settlement had been rooted. Together, the girls put him comfortably on a section of a log that had been rolled up beside the fire pit. No blaze burned there now, but when she saw the old man shiver, Ayina nodded to Teala. The girl set aside her weaving and moved toward the tumble of deadfall waiting for the fire.

But Netah shook her head. "There are men in the canyon below us," she whispered. "There is no smoke for them to smell, and they should not know that we are here."

Teala glanced at Ayina, who nodded. The girl went

inside the hut and brought out a robe, which she wrapped about the old man. He hugged it around his shoulders and turned to the older woman.

"Men? In the canyon? Have they come to take away the granddaughters?" His voice was strained with tension.

"No," Ayina murmured into his ear. "These are strangers, if Netah is correct. Go into your hut, Sekto. We will watch, and if need be we will protect you."

Mumbling, the old man moved toward his small lodge, while Ayina and Teala visited their own and returned armed with short lances. The trees were too thick to waste arrows, but once an enemy was close by a lance was a very useful weapon. Each also carried a leather sling, for rocks abounded for ammunition, if there was need for such.

For once, the old men surprised Ayina. As she tied her skirtlike garment about her hips to keep it from brushing against the bushes, she heard a quiet movement. Turning, she saw the four standing beside her own lodge. Each was armed, and Sekto, no longer dim and fumbling, seemed to have found focus and sharpness that he had lacked for many moons.

Pahket leaned forward. "We cannot climb well, but we will guard this camp. You who are young must go down to make certain these are not enemies, come to destroy us."

Ayina understood his concern. Together they had seen the work of the Tsununni, the fall of their people's houses that had seemed so strong. Enemies had begun their later lives by destroying their homes and their families, leaving them alone in a harsh world that seemed intent upon destroying even their lives.

Ayina smiled at the four, so feeble and yet so indomitable. "Yes. It is good, for there are only the four of us to watch all the approaches to our home. Keep guard, my friends, and we will see who is in the canyon and what they are about."

She did not have to instruct her granddaughters. They knew from childhood their duties in such a situation. Wordless, silent on their cautious feet, the girls moved upslope, along the path leading around the belly of the mountain, and down to the right.

Ayina took the left-hand way, moving down as silently as a ferret toward the distant river that wound at the bottom of the cleft between these green-clad mountains. She brushed past scarlet flowers that grew from cracks in a boulder, through the tender green of berry bushes and saplings leaning out into the free sunlight over the gulf below.

The trees grew tall, and she used their thick trunks to steady herself as she moved onto the steepest part of the slope. At last she lay flat and edged downward, holding with toes and elbows in the rich mulch dropped by generations of hardwoods and conifers.

There was a rocky runnel where snowmelt ran away down the mountain into the river. She found its shallow groove and slid into it, moving more freely in its concealment. When it came to the verge of the last cliff overhanging the stream some three man-heights above the water, she stopped short of the lip and laid her head flat on the ground, slipping forward through the trickle of water until she risked one eye's width to peer into the bottom of the canyon.

Ayina saw nothing, but her keen ears caught a splash that did not sound like the normal rush of waters from their high source. She remained frozen in place, that watching eye scanning the thick greenery lining the banks of the river.

There came a grunt, a word spoken in a deep but hushed voice. They were coming, those intruders into the high country. Hunters, perhaps, or men looking for new fishing spots. But any stranger was probably an enemy.

They came into sight, three short, square-shouldered men carrying bows slung about their backs. Each held a thick staff, with which they examined the bushes through which they traveled. When they came to the eddy above the sharp bend in the river, they probed the deep hole pooled behind the boulder that contained it.

One man laid aside his weapons and walked into the water, probing ahead with a length of sapling as if searching for something hidden beneath the surface. The rest watched the growth on their side of the stream, checking behind rocks and clumps of bushes and in thickets of alder or pine.

They were searching for something—or someone. It could not be her people, for these were men she had never seen before. Had a captive escaped from some village far down in the valley? It seemed almost certain.

Ayina watched until the searchers moved out of sight, still going upriver, still probing and prying and sniffing in every spot that might offer concealment. Then she slid backward up the runnel, moving silently and painfully over the rocks that lined the gully. When she was again among the thick growth of trees, she edged out of her hiding place and stood upright in the shadows, wondering about those she had seen below.

From above came the clear call of a magpie, and she knew that one of the young women had seen those beneath them turn to go back the way they had come. As she went upward again, moving rather painfully now that the urgency had left her, she heard a sudden silence among the insects that had been humming and chirruping quietly in the sun-warmed greenery about her.

Startled, she looked around sharply. As she gazed into the depths of a squat bush, she found her heart jump in her breast. A pair of bright black eyes stared back at her from a small, dark face.

She was, she had no doubt, looking into the eyes of a child for whom the men along the river had been searching.

❧4❧

Spring had filled the puma with restless energy. He had hunted out his high terrain, making the long loop that was his usual course at that time of year. Now he headed down into the grasslands, his mouth watering after one of the sleek beasts that grazed there, already fat on the grass of that warmer country.

He avoided the stinking place where the hunters lived, for he had learned in his youth that the two-legged predators were dangerous, working, like wolves, in packs. But driven by spring madness, he drank from a spring running down near the rounded lodges, and there he came eye to eye with one of their young.

He turned instantly and fled toward the hills and the forest. He had escaped them many times, and he had no doubt he would escape from them again. That night he shifted his course still more to the north, feeling certain that he was now safe.

The net that caught him was a shocking surprise. He had come down to drink in the twilight, after sitting for a long while on a high knoll and watching the broken land

30

leading down to the little stream he had chosen. Yet those two-legs managed to trap him, the oldest, wisest puma in the mountains, and roll him into their net as if he were a yearling cub.

Snarling, occasionally giving a coughing cry, he felt himself lifted and carried, his back to the ground, his face staring up at a pole and beyond it the darkening sky. Being a puma, he did not wonder what was going to happen to him. That sort of worry was not a part of his heritage.

Instead, he felt his rage grow as he was carried along and found himself at last in the smoke-smelling center of the huddle of lodges. His captors gave him no chance to show his anger, however. They pushed him, still tangled in the net, into a pole cage and bound the door-flap fast with thongs, leaving him to work his way free if he could.

Once he was alone, except for the small meat that poked a stick at him through the poles of his cage, the puma rolled onto his belly and began worrying at the fibers of the net. Soon he had his head free, and not long after that he had bitten through the cords and the rest of the net and stood, shaking himself, lashing his tail, and giving voice to his outrage.

Even the slash of his steely claws did not open the door, however, and in time he lay flat, his tongue lolling as he panted. Narrowing his eyes, he watched through slitted pupils the movements of the creatures that had taken him from his hunt.

When meat came bouncing into his cage through a hole in the top, he nosed it cautiously. But his pride would not allow him to touch that, yet. Hunger would, in time, bring him to eat from the hands of these creatures, for he was *eminently practical. But for the moment he was content to observe them.*

Day came, and night again. In time, the puma took the meat they had given him. The sun came and went, came and went, and his impatience changed to sullen waiting. Something in his wild spirit told him that things might change. Something began to compel him toward an invisible goal he had no way to comprehend.

There was, beside the place where he was confined, another cage, smaller, tighter. In the evening, some days later, there came a party of men carrying a small meat that was not one of their own. It struggled and bit and kicked, still, but it was too little to succeed against those who were so much larger.

The puma flicked his ears and concentrated his gaze on the creature the men fastened into the cage beside his own. When the captors went away, again the small meat of the village came to poke sticks through the poles at this other one, so like them and yet so different.

It sat up and caught one of the sticks, jerked it into the cage, and jabbed it outward, catching one of its tormentors in the belly. That one howled and the others ran away quickly. The captive meat made a strange sound, half whoop, half sob, and lay on its face, its shoulders shaking.

Strange. The cougar went to sleep considering its fellow captive.

Again, day followed day. From time to time a group of the men came to stand beside the cages, making the sounds they used among themselves. The puma was not interested, but he saw that the other captive listened intently.

On the last night of his captivity, a tall man, robed in fur and feathers, came and talked very loudly to those who followed him. Even the puma realized that something important was happening, although, being what he was, he did not concern himself with it.

Yet in the night he heard secret scratchings and clicks, and he woke to see the small meat beside him chew through the last of the bindings on his cage and go free through the door. That brought the puma onto his paws, head lowered, his eyes glowing with the intensity of his desire to escape, too.

That little creature, which had done a thing the puma had not been able to do, stood for a moment, staring into the cage. Then one hand rose and jerked at something the puma could not see.

At once the small shape darted away into the darkness making no sound, arousing no alarm as it fled. When it was out of sight, the puma dabbed at the door of his own cage with one tentative paw. It swung silently open, and, feeling the freedom of the heights in the smell of the wind, he fled like a shadow across the village and into the hills along the river.

The boy sank instantly into the bush that almost concealed him, but Ayina moved far more quickly than she had thought possible. She pounced upon him and caught a thin wrist to drag him out into the open.

Small and skinny, he wore nothing except a complete set of scratches and bruises. His flight had probably caused the scratches, but she felt certain that those from whom he had fled might well have provided the purplish patches that splotched his dark skin.

He said nothing, though there was terror in the eyes that stared up at her, the whites visible around the dark irises. She shook her head and pointed downward toward the river, now far below and out of sight behind the intervening trees. Then she released the small arm and stepped back, setting aside her lance and raising her empty hands.

She turned and took up the lance again, using its length to help her climb the steep slope. Behind her she heard hesitant padding steps as the child followed, and she smiled to herself. This young one, whoever he might be, whatever his people, could only be welcome in her small camp.

When she came to the main deer track along the mountainside, Ayina whistled the sharp call of a jay. Twice then once, that was the signal to warn others that she was coming back. She did not follow the trail but slid through the thick growth alongside it, up the slope where an outcrop of rock took no tracks.

The little boy froze in place, she noted from the corner of her eye, until she moved again. Then, very hesitantly, he crept forward almost to her heels.

She turned to look down at him. When his gaze met hers she allowed a tiny smile to touch her lips. Then she reached her free hand toward him. He stared at it for a moment before taking her fingers in his and moving along the narrow edge just behind her, his arm at full stretch.

Teala met her before the lodge, and soon Netah and Pulap joined them. The old men rose from the bushes where they had hidden in ambush against any intruder who approached their homes. They stared at the boy, wordless. Indeed, no one said anything for a long moment.

Then Ayina sat down on a chunk of wood and gestured for the child to stand before her. "Who are your people?" she asked him. "Where have you come from?"

It was obvious that he did not understand the tongue of the Geh-i-nah. But he seemed bright, and he hunkered down at her feet and drew a wiggly line in the dust. She had a sudden memory of doing the same, far back when she was a child confronted with an alien people.

He pointed down, and she knew he meant this to be the river. Then he waved an arm downstream. He drew in a rough circle, which might have been the village of his captors or might not.

He took a twig and carefully smoothed the dust so that it lay flat. That was clear enough; he lived in the flatlands beyond the mountains. Into that flatness, he again drew the river, digging the twig in deeply to make what must be a fairly deep canyon. There he drew a smaller circle.

His own people's village? Perhaps he was from one of the tribes living below the mountains, in the valleys to the east. It seemed reasonable to think so.

She touched her face. "Ayina," she said. "Ayina."

He looked at her intently. Then he pointed to Sekto, who stood very near.

"Sekto," Ayina told him. "Sekto."

He nodded. "Ish-o-tobi," he said. "Ish-o-tobi. Tuali-rani."

She nodded. It was enough for now; she knew that, being so young, he would learn to communicate quickly. She had seen other captive children, over the years of her life, assimilate smoothly into a new tribe.

Her people had dwindled rapidly, for it seemed in later years that few of those of an age to have children could produce offspring. They had stolen children or gathered in lost ones as often as possible.

Now it remained to see if those who hunted this small one intended to range up into the mountains on either side of the river before they ended their search.

Teala was convinced that the three men had gone back downstream, but Ayina was not certain of that. In hunting for a child, any wise person would deceive the quarry into thinking himself safe. Then the hunter would surprise him and bear him away into captivity again.

Yet she wondered why there was such an intensive search for this particular young one. Few of the people she had encountered from other kinds seemed to value small ones until they reached an age to be of value in hunting or other tribal tasks.

A sudden thought made her glance down again at the starved shape at her feet. "Could he be a sacrifice to some god of hunters?" she asked her companions, who looked puzzled.

Ayina felt impatient, but she explained. "Those lowlanders stalk the great beasts that roam the plains. Once when I was very young a man of the Geh-i-nah was sent to such a tribe with some message I did not understand at the time. He returned with fascinating stories about their hunts and their customs. He had seen a child used so, sent to the Buffalo Gods in return for the beasts they hoped to kill.

"But this is only guesswork. Now, it is worth considering the possibility that those who searched along the river were engaged in more important matters than a quest for an escaped slave-child. What if Isho-tobi was meant to be part of a religious ritual? That would mean those men will not give up easily."

Sekto, roused from his apathy by this new possibility of danger, turned his dim gaze upon Ayina. "If they search the mountainside, they will find this place. We are four men and four women, and there are three lodges. If only we who are very old and seem unable to be a danger to them are found here, it may be that they will think us alone on the mountain.

"The forest and the slopes contain places where we could hide many hands of people without the possibility of their being discovered. If you, Ayina, and the young women go up into the high places, taking the child with you—carrying him, so that no track of his small foot will show—then there will be no chance that you will have to fight those who are coming."

"But they are strangers, probably enemies," Ayina said. "If they learn you are here, they may kill you."

"We are old," Sekto said. "Life is sweet, but not one of us has much of it left to spend. It is better to die as a man, fighting an enemy, than to slip away in a dream and never to know you are dead until you find yourself walking in the Other Place."

"No." Ayina felt the wisdom of the elder's plan, but she was also unwilling to abandon her charges to such a fate. "The girls will take the child and go up toward the great stone peak beyond the meadows at the top of

this mountain. I will remain hidden, armed and ready
to defend you. There are only three of them, so far. If
they find you and kill you and return to their own
place, who knows if others may not come up the river
to see if you were, indeed, the only ones living on the
slopes?"

Teala stepped forward, her eyes blazing indignant-
ly. "We do not want to run and hide, while you who
have sheltered us and taught us and kept us safe all
our lives face the danger that belongs to all of us," the
girl said. "I will remain with you and watch, too."

But Ayina shook her head. "You have made a promise to the young man who will come to meet you in
a few moons, now. Your training is valuable and not
to be wasted before you have had the time to use it
for your new family. No, Teala, you and Pulap and
Netah must go upward, now. Lift the child and carry
him away, for I feel the approach of intruders into our
long peace."

Teala opened her mouth to speak, but a bird called
around the shoulder of the mountain, and another took
up the tale. Walkers were coming. Without another
word, she lifted Ish-o-tobi and moved upward, taking
the difficult slope in stride instead of going the longer
route by way of the game track.

The other girls followed her, carrying their lances
and their slings. When they were out of sight, Ayina
went into her house and took from a leather wrapping
the atlatl that she had made when first she came into
this green country. The missiles were there, the carefully chipped points still solid on the wooden shafts.

"I will watch from the great boulder that crops
out of the cliff above our village," she said, when

she emerged to face the old men. "I wish you well, Sekto, Eketan, Pahket, Abani. We have been kinsmen for many seasons. I would wish that we may be friends for several more."

She forgot the stiffness of her knees, the pain in her joints as she made her way up and around to her chosen perch, which was concealed by thick bushes growing about the base of the boulder. Once she was in place, she twittered like a nesting bird, and, below her, Sekto nodded.

Ayina watched the old men scuff out the smaller tracks of the women and the child. They trampled over the flat space among the lodges with their withered feet, as if only they had moved there since the last rain. Then they went into the lodges, Sekto into her own, Pahket and Abani into the second, and Eketan into the third.

Lying flat on the gritty rock, Ayina smiled. They were, with all their faults, all their grumbling and demands upon her time and effort, a brave little band of men, still willing to die for their people. She could never have left them to face this danger alone.

She listened closely as disturbed birds and displaced small animals warned of the approach of the newcomers to the mountain. Now there was the pad of feet in the dust of the game trail that she had carefully avoided using when she brought the child to her home. The searchers were coming.

When they were close enough below the boulder to be hidden from her, she slithered forward to the edge of the stone and risked an eye's width to see what happened beneath the overhang. The first of the searchers paused when he saw the rude lodges built on the small apron of flat ground interrupting the mountainside.

He gestured; his companions nocked arrows to their short bows and stepped aside, one going down to flank the little village from below, the other hugging the cliff on which she waited, out of sight beneath the bulge of her own concealing boulder. The leader darted forward, bow ready, and pushed aside the door-flap of her lodge.

In a moment, he came out dragging Sekto behind him. He flung the old man to the ground, his attitude showing his contempt for this ancient bag of bones. The other man left the concealment of the boulder and went to check the second lodge, and the third climbed from below and went into the remaining hut.

In a moment, all of the elders were huddled together near the fire pit, their heads bowed, their thin legs drawn up into angles of sticklike bones. Each, she saw with satisfaction, wore his deer-hide robe against the cool of the heights. Beneath, she knew without checking, each had concealed a knife. They would not go alone into the Other Place, if it came to a battle.

The leader of the searchers was bending, studying the dust about the lodges. But evidently the old men had done their work well, and he shook his head in disgust as he returned to his fellows.

The leader, who was a bit taller and somewhat heavier than the other two, reached into the string knife-sling at his waist and brought out a flint knife whose quality Ayina could see even from a distance.

That was the signal to kill these strange old men, leaving no possible enemy on the mountain.

Ayina stood on her boulder and whipped her atlatl with deadly accuracy. Her missile struck the strange chief between the shoulder-blades; he went flat and lay with only a faint twitch of his legs to show his death.

Before she could hook another arrow onto the leading tip of the atlatl, the Geh-i-nah elders below rose from their submissive huddle and busied their knives in the flesh of the other two, who seemed stunned for an instant at the unexpected fall of their leader. Before she could drop from the edge of the boulder, all three were lying in their own blood, their blank eyes staring in astonishment at the spring sky.

She stood beside Eketan, feeling his old body shake, hearing the harshness of his breathing. The other three men were panting as well, for it had been a very long while since any of them had put forth such strenuous effort.

"You have done well," Ayina said. "But now we have a new problem. Where these came, others may well follow, seeking for the seekers.

"When the girls return, and they will come before nightfall, I think, we must pack up everything we need, take down these houses that have served us for so long, and go into the high country. There must be nothing here, no bodies, no trace of people of any kind, to tell those who come searching that anyone has ever set a foot upon this side of the river."

Sekto nodded. "It is hard to move, when you are old. But you are right. We will have to find how to meet with those who come for their brides, but young

men have a special sense when it comes to finding
young women. We will go, and they will come, when
the time is right."

He stared down at the fallen strangers and sighed.
"I would like to have known who their people are,
what their names might be. Alone here for so long, I
have been starved for the tales of strangers. It is sad
that men, few as we are, must meet always as enemies
in this wide land."

Ayina had never thought of that before, but it was
true. Why could not the few tribes inhabiting these
rich lands share their words and their skills?

But it was only through great effort that she had
made contact with those of the Ahye-tum-datsehe
who were to marry her granddaughters. Otherwise,
the girls might have lived out their lives, unwed and
without children, on this forest-furred mountain.

❧5❧

After a time Teala whistled from above, her call indistinguishable from that of a hunting hawk. Ayina replied in kind, and in a few moments all three girls, trailed by the stranger child, came down into the village and looked about them.

It took few words to explain what must be done. Then everyone busied themselves with packing their scanty goods, dismantling and clearing away the bark and pole lodges, and hiding the components by scattering them amid tangles of deadfall and thickets of bushes all along the side of the mountain.

Ayina and Netah wrapped the dead men in deer hides, which contained any blood that still flowed, and dragged them, one by one, to an overhang of rock far down the slope and around the shoulder of the mountain. When all three were laid in a row, their weapons, even the fine flint knife, were placed beside them. The two women dug at the base of the overhang until the stone ledge was loosened. Netah jumped on top and bounced there, pushing it down and down until, with a sigh and a grating, the ledge began to move. The girl leaped lightly aside, allowing the great chunk of stone and soil to descend on the strangers, covering them beyond hope of discovery.

Ayina, watching, felt strangely sad. But she did not allow that to divert her alertness as she checked the area, brushing away any mark in soil or leaf-mulch. Together, she and Netah moved back toward their campsite, removing as they went any trace of the dragging bodies or their own human presence.

They found that their companions had been busy. There was no trace of pole or bark, not even a hole where the supports had been footed. No fire pit could be found, and any ash had been removed and replaced with drifts of last year's leaves, decayed branches from the trees overhanging the spot, and artful bird tracks, made with carefully shaped twigs.

Ayina was pleased. No seeker after those dead men would ever suspect their fate. She hoped devoutly they would never dream that other men than they walked the mountain, for she had no desire to kill more people whose names she did not know. The arrival of the fierce Tsununni, which had ended her life as one of the great Geh-i-nah community, had given her both a distrust of strangers and an aversion to dealing out death.

She sent the others on ahead, noting with interest that the child had attached himself to Sekto and walked just behind the old man, helping him to carry his bundles of possessions.

When her people were out of sight up the mountain, Ayina checked once again, noting and removing every trace of a footprint, any sign of a dragging hide or pole. When she swung herself up by an overhanging branch, not even her own footprint was left in the dust that had held her home.

She was exhausted, but she trudged after her people, still noticing and covering up any trace of their passing. Her legs ached, her back pained her as she bent beneath her own burden of hides and pots and weapons, but she ignored the protests of her body. Survival was important; pain was not. Old habit kept her moving until she caught up with the group that had paused to allow the old men to rest.

The three girls lay comfortably on the pine straw beneath a thick clump of trees. Sekto sat on a fallen log, holding Ish-o-tobi in his lap. Eketan lay on his face, snoring. Pahket sat beside him, his shrewd eyes keeping watch on everything and everyone.

Abani leaned against a tree, his face ashen, holding his painful arms against his chest. She knew that his twisted joints were giving him agony and that he had been moving by willpower alone.

They had traveled a very respectable distance for people so old and weary, Ayina thought. Yet they must go on still until they found a place in which it was safe to camp and build a fire. They must have solid food tonight; as soon as they stopped she would send one of the girls out to find a woodchuck or deer or other game. Only enough food would keep her people going for long enough to find a new homeplace.

But first she must rest. The sun was sinking behind the mountain now, and the sky was growing dark above the pine tops. If she had been ten summers younger, she would have pushed them all forward,

but now she knew that her own limbs would not continue without rest.

Ayina put aside her burden and lay flat beside
Eketan. It was growing chill as evening crept forward, and his warmth beside her was a comfort as
she sank into a light doze. Age was a merciless thing,
she thought as she relaxed. It took the will from your
heart, even as it sapped strength from muscle and
bone.

It seemed that she could have had no time to sleep,
for almost at once she woke to a firm hand on her
shoulder, shaking her gently. "It is time to go on,
Grandmother," Teala's voice murmured in her ear.
"I have killed two grouse, and we will have food
when we stop for the night, but it seems to me that
we should go even farther upward before we stop. I
feel that someone will come soon, in the steps of those
left below."

Ayina sat and retied the thong holding her long
twist of hair in place. "You are right," she said. "I
should not have slept at all. It is as well that you
and the others are going away to a people who have
younger and more alert watchers and warriors."

Already the other two girls were helping the old
men position their burdens. Without asking, Teala
added much of Ayina's own load to her own and put
more into the frames carried by Netah and Pulap.

"If you are to carry my things, then I will carry the
child," the old woman said, noting the drooping head
of the little boy. "He is too young to stay awake for so
long."

When they went upward again, she came behind,
the child's light body held to her back with a length

of deer hide, his head lolling against her. It was a familiar and pleasant thing, reminding her of a time when her own children were small enough to carry.

As she walked through the dappled darkness of the slanting forest, aided in her journey by the flecks or moonlight striking down through the spreading branches and new leaves, she thought of her children. Sohala, eldest daughter; Nitipu, firstborn son; Setichi, second and dearest son; Tilepita, youngest daughter and adored infant.

It had been a very long time since their deaths, and the harsh life of outcasts had overlaid their memories. Now, again cast out of what had become familiar surroundings, Ayina found herself grieving once again for her lost ones.

Why had her people not listened as she warned that such an attack was possible? She pushed away the thought. There were present dangers that she must deal with. The past was there in the west, with her lost people.

The moon was rising, and she used the patches of light to check for traces of her people's feet in the leaves and rocky soil underfoot. The child grew heavy, but she did not slow. They must reach a proper camping spot before she and the old men dropped, unable to move again.

The mountaintops, she knew, still held snow, but the air no longer held the bitter chill of winter. Although Ayina avoided the river, knowing that those pursuing the child might come that far when they found no trace of him below, she kept to the edges of the forest that came down to the wide, flat stretches lying along its now narrow course.

Ahead, from time to time, she could see against the paler sky the tall shape of the peak that crowned this mountain. Bare rock, it stood amid the flatter reaches that stretched away at its foot. Ayina thought that there might be good summer camping there in the tangles of trees she recalled from her earliest explorations of all the parts of this mountain she had chosen for her people.

The going was much easier once they came to this level country, and small game was abundant, coming out of burrows into the new spring. At last, both darkness and exhaustion overtook her group, and they paused in the shelter of a rocky nook.

The grouse that Teala had killed were soon spitted on an alder branch and turning over the small fire kindled in the concealment of the stones. The smoke was carried away up the tall chimney created by the split in the cliff that had created their shelter. Anyone hunting or seeking herbs here so early might sniff the smoke, but it would be dispersed over so much area that there would be no way of locating its source.

They ate ravenously. Then the young ones portioned out the watches of the night, and their elders lay gratefully on their deer-hide blankets and fell into deep sleep. Ayina held the child cuddled against her body, and the feeling was warm and familiar as he slept deeply, as only children can.

Ayina jerked herself into wakefulness when Netah touched her shoulder. The sky above the cleft was still dark, but the scent of dawn was in the air. She sat and woke the child; then she reached to touch Eketan's back. His groan told her that he was awake, and she knew he would rouse his fellows.

Before the sky lightened, they were moving again, after covering all trace of their camp and the fire. Now Ayina found her memory of this high part of the mountain coming back strongly. Each pale-boled hardwood seemed to greet her, and the pines seemed familiar.

For three days and nights they traveled, and on the fourth morning they stood amid the forest beyond which lay the stream dividing it from the forbidding rock crowning the height. Snow lay on the north sides of trees and in the deep shade of the pines and blue-tinged firs. Bushes had not yet leafed out, but shoots and pale leaves of plants were pushing upward underfoot.

The air was clean and sharp, and Ayina drew in great lungfuls of it, as if it were medicine that might make her young again. "This is a good place," she said. "I remember thinking so when I came here first, when you children were still small ones. I have kept it in my mind since, thinking that if we needed to move our home, this would be a fine summer hiding place."

Sekto dropped to sit on his bundle of possessions. "It is very far," he sighed. "But that is good, when enemies may be hunting for us. Where will we build our lodges? There is plenty of wood, and I have seen a handful of mule deer since we woke this morning. Hides and poles will be easy to find."

That brought on a discussion about the best location, but Ayina ignored it. She closed her eyes and turned her head, trying to find the right feeling of direction.

There had been a game track, very near this place, that followed a creek branching away from the main stream. The forest was thick there, the water close by, the wind held away by the bulwark of the peak beyond the trees.

As she turned, feeling rather than looking for the proper course, she caught a scent that she had forgotten she knew. The combination of firs and pines was just right. It was this way. . . .

She left the earnest group of Geh-i-nah and slipped into the narrow track, bending to miss the low curves of branches that had shaped themselves to the height of the deer who made this path. After a few paces, the way opened out and she stood erect, looking up into the tops of tall trees whose spring buds gleamed in the sunlight. Blue spruce surrounded a little glade, at the farther end of which a spring chuckled from beneath a big rock and purled away in loops toward the creek that was some distance away, though the mutter of its waters was quite audible in the quiet.

This was a good place. A place of peace. Perhaps even a place of safety, in which she could build new lodges and shelter her people until the danger posed by those alien people passed. Without any warning, a small hand pushed into hers, and she looked down at Ish-o-tobi, who had followed her so quietly that she had not known he was behind her.

"My house will be there," she said, looking into a clump of bushes that promised to bear berries, in time. "And we will build it large enough for all of us. It will be soon enough when we old ones are left alone. The old men will be happy to be surrounded with life, for the short time left to us."

Then she turned back the way she had come, the boy's small hand held firmly. Ayina was ready to bring her people into this hidden spot that promised to hide them and keep them safe.

⯮6⯯

The lodge that Ayina proposed to build for her extended family was to be much larger than their simple huts in the lower country. As high as they now were, it was likely that they would see snow even in summer, and winter would be bitter, if it proved necessary for them to remain there for so long.

Having the entire group under the same roof, warmed by the same fuel, seemed the most sensible way to house them. Ayina surveyed the chosen spot, her mind racing with possibilities.

She stepped off five paces, using a sapling behind her as one end of her invisible line and marking the other with the sharp stake she carried for that purpose. She stabbed the stake solidly into the spring-soft ground, and to it she secured a length of thong, which she measured out carefully. Then, walking around the central stake, she drew on the ground with another sharp stick, forming a circle.

That would be the shape of this house. She set Teala to measuring the distance between the supports, which would be footed deeply in the ground. At the center she put Pahket digging with a stick to loosen the earth that must be moved.

Except for short hunting trips after woodchucks and grouse and deer, the Geh-i-nah labored for days. Isho-tobi, grown fatter now with plenty of food, helped with digging a central pit into the middle of which the support post was set. They spaced the outer supports around the circumference of the circle, and laid saplings to support the roof, angling them from the crotch of the center to the forks of the posts.

The interior was sunk some eight hands into the ground. Its roof of poles was covered with fir thatch, over which they began the laborious task of forming a thick layer of soil. Along the stream, Ayina found layers of flat stones, which she painfully excavated and broke into sections to carry upward. Those formed the fire pit, which was offset from the center post, positioned beneath a hole that had been carefully shaped into the earth cover to carry away smoke.

In a hand of days the house was finished, its shape much like that of a mushroom, the solid earthen top sloping down to the ground to form a draft-free enclosure. The door was on the south side, protected by a short tunnel that hid any light from the fire from possible intruders. This would, in winter, prevent drafts from bringing in the chill from outside.

This was the best house Ayina had known since the Tsununni destroyed the stone house of her clan, back in the west, where the country was even higher and the canyons so deep that they had been considered sound protection from enemies. She leaned against the post in the center of the house and stared about the shadowy interior, the spot of sunlight beneath the smoke hole, the neat layers of stone waiting for the first fire.

Ayina felt a great sense of relief. She had not realized how much she had missed the feeling of solid walls around her, all those years when she had lived in that flimsy hut above the river. Her people had built solidly and well, and only the Tsununni had been able, at last, to force their survivors away from their homes above their canyon . . . but she did not allow herself to think about that.

"All this work," Pahket grumbled from the shadows behind her. "If you had left that young one where you found him, we would still be in our old houses, for surely those men would never have come so high to look for him."

That was Pahket, always complaining, always saying sharp things that hurt. Yet he, almost as much as Sekto, seemed to be fond of the child. Ayina didn't trouble to answer him, for they both knew that one never could predict what hunters would do, even when they hunted elk or deer or moose. When men hunted man, it was even more perilous to guess.

Ayina pushed away the memories that had troubled her mind. There was no time to think of the past or to worry about the future, except to try to prepare for any danger it was possible to foresee. Having lived so long and suffered so much from just such unexpected perils, Ayina found it hard to keep from worrying about the future.

But she stooped to leave through the tunnel-like entrance and stood outside in the fragrant air of the mountaintop. The wind sang in the fir needles, and the soil was soft underfoot. From the concealment of the glade she could see nothing except the top of the loaf-shaped peak beyond the forest and the sky itself, domed in blue depths above her, its streaks of cirrus cloud promising weather to come.

Good. That might keep any searchers at home or in camp. She was not certain that those who had sent the dead men would be content to lose them, as well as the child, without further effort. From what she could learn from Ish-o-tobi, Ayina was convinced that he had been intended as a sacrifice to some god or to the great horned beasts that lived in the grasslands. The tales she had heard in her old life indicated that was probable.

She had never involved herself in the rituals of the shamans of her people. Being a skeptic by nature, she felt that those gods who showed themselves in storm and thunder, mountains and clouds and sun, would pay no heed to the puny chants and drawings and drummings of any people, even her own.

In her heart she felt a strong connection to plants and to animals, as well as to the people she had saved. Other than her need to help her own and to use the things about her to best advantage, she had no particular patience with religion. She could not guess how strongly it drove those who lived in the rich valleys below the mountain she had chosen for a refuge.

It was good that this house was so well hidden, she thought as she crept through the firs and moved entirely around its location. She had cautioned the wary young women about making trails where none had been before. The old men, sleepy and absentminded

as they were, knew in their bones about such things
as well.

Except for rabbit trails, deer tracks, the big hoof
marks of elk, she found no trace of man. The game
trails her people used were best avoided. They must
come and go by different ways every time they left
the glade. That was not a bad idea at any time, and
only their location on the steep slopes lower on the
mountain had dictated use of the natural approaches
to their camp.

*The night wind riffled the puma's fur as he ran. No man
was visible as he left the village behind and headed for the
river that wound upward into the forested mountains. He
paused to drink from the stream before he turned along a
faint track that held the prints of hooves and paws and the
claws of birds.*

*He was free, and the very air beckoned to him as he
moved, now with easy assurance, toward his distant goal.
He would leave behind this lower country, moving into the
higher ranges. There was prey enough there, though not so
fat, and he would be far from those who had netted him and
carried him into captivity.*

*He slept, in time, beneath a boulder that formed a shelf
above a steep incline. When he rose again he felt so secure
that he slid into the open and sauntered down the slope
toward water.*

*The murky liquid they had set before him in that cage had
been dreadful stuff, gritty and stinking. The chill freshness
of the river drew him again to a spot where the path ran
close beside the stream.*

*An arrow caught him in the flank as he bent his head
toward the water, and he sprang aside into the brush, spit-*

ting feline curses. The thing dragged at him, catching on twigs and tree trunks, but the puma did not stop to worry it loose from his hide. He knew that he must flee for his life, for the enemy was now too close at hand.

He ran, dropping bright specks of blood along his way, until he came to an overhang of stone, on which he stood panting, looking back along the way he had come. He heard a whistle. Knowing that they would follow him closely, now that he was wounded, he sprang out and down, spitting as he sank into the icy water.

But he swam strongly against the current, and in time he emerged on the other shore and slunk along in the shadow of the overhang of bushes and boulders to a spot where he could lie down. He curled his tawny body back on itself and bit desperately at the wooden shaft.

It crackled and splintered, and most of the wood fell away. The flint point was still a constant agony in his muscle, and blood still flowed, though now it was beginning to slow. Limping heavily, the cat crept along until he found a way to climb higher. Then, his tongue lolling, his sides heaving, he moved with painful determination toward the places that called him toward their cool, safe heights.

Ayina stared off across the wide stretch of grassland and scrub that slanted to the larger creek downslope. Five mule deer browsed on the foliage among the bushes, and above an eagle circled, its call sharp in the cool air.

Even as she watched, the buck raised its head and stared downstream. The two does faded into the brush, followed by their fawns. Then the buck whirled and bounced away upstream. Something had alarmed him and the does. Was someone coming along the water?

She could not take a chance of having her people surprised. Ayina checked for footprints in the grass where she had been standing, but her soft moccasins left no mark. Then she turned and slipped through the thick growth that covered the higher land along the creek, retracing her steps until she stood again beside the new house.

There she called three times, the shrill *skree* of a hawk. That was the signal they had arranged among them to warn of danger. Soon Teala came into view, carrying a basket of herbs newly gleaned from the high forest. Netah and Pulap came from the small spring, their pots filled with water.

Three of the old men appeared from the fir thicket, and Ish-o-tobi tagged after them, carrying a huge armload of fir tips to be boiled for tea or to soften the beds of those with old bones.

Ayina gestured for silence. Then she pointed toward the lower country. Her hand mimicked the flight of the buck, the subtle disappearance of the does and fawns. She stared upward, hoping the eagle would be in sight, and he was, almost beyond the forest tops but visible.

He was circling widely, evidently interested in something taking place below him. It was the intruder, whatever it had been, she was certain. She gestured toward the house, and her people followed her into its chilly shelter. She was glad they had not yet kindled a fire in the pit, for smoke would give away their presence, if those were kinsmen of the men they had killed.

Huddled with the rest inside the thick mud walls of the house, Ayina explained the disturbance observed lower on the mountain. "The eagle saw something, I know, for he tightened his circle and tilted his wing to allow him to see more clearly. Some danger, human or animal, is on the mountain, and the buck ran upstream, as if to escape it."

There was a pause, while the Geh-i-nah thought hard of ways to learn what this might be and how to deal with it. Ayina had an uneasy feeling the valley people might have sent large numbers to avenge the deaths of their trackers.

Eketan sat beside the pool of light sifting down through the smoke hole. The warm reflections on his withered face turned it into a mask, from which his eyes gleamed in the dimness. "We must go and see. Our people once tried retreating into a strong place for protection, and you remember, Ayina, what happened then."

She nodded. The old man was right. The strong houses, even positioned strategically as they were, had not saved her people, and this mud-cloaked pit house would not even stop a bear that was determined to claw its way inside. Only the fact that in winter the bears would be asleep would allow her people to survive the snow season here.

"We must go and see what is coming," Teala said, and her companions nodded their agreement. "If trackers come, they will find some trace, however careful we have been, and we will be trapped here, to be killed as we come out at last, starved and thirsty."

"You are right," Ayina agreed. "Who will go with me to scout along the stream? Some must remain here, for Ish-o-tobi must not be left alone, nor can Abani manage to go so far and then have strength to return. Sekto's eyes are dim and he would have trouble seeing, even if he went. They should stay near our house, but well hidden in the forest."

Sekto sighed. "I will keep the dogs quiet," he said, and she knew that he, better than any, could control the animals and keep them from betraying the presence of their masters.

Eketan straightened his thin shoulders and grinned, turning his face into a map of wrinkles. Pahket reached for his bow and stood, not grumbling for once, ready to leave at need.

There was no good purpose served by waiting. Ayina armed herself and joined Teala and Netah outside. Pulap said, "I will remain here with the others. There may be need for someone who can run fast and see well."

Soon the five Geh-i-nah were moving cautiously through the thickest forest, slipping from fir to spruce to pine, from shadow to shadow, flitting so softly and unobtrusively that Ayina knew even the eagle to be unaware of their passing. When they came to the first downward slope commanding the meadow beside the stream below, she sent Teala up a tree to observe what was taking place there.

She lay flat with the others, waiting, listening. She could hear a distant hawk, the occasional cry of the eagle, squeaks and small sounds from the lesser creatures inhabiting the high places.

Leaves whispered against needled branches, and in the distance she heard the yip of a fox. Her heart freezing, she listened, but no excited yelps told of the Geh-i-nah dogs, far above in the trees beside Sekto.

She lay, chin on fist, watching the sunlit meadows,

noting every motion of the wind in the grass, the sway of branches in the tall trees lining the watercourse. A large rabbit burst out of the bushes beneath those and bounded desperately across the grass, disappearing in its depths, only to bob into sight at the top of every spring.

Above her in the tree, Teala hissed just loudly enough to be heard over the breeze among the needles. Then, without any sound to warn of her coming, she was beside Ayina.

"Puma," she mouthed, as her grandmother turned to look into her face. "Very large. But sick or injured, I think. I thought I could see blood on its flank."

If her people had been the kind to utter useless curses, Ayina might have cursed then. An arrow would mean a human hunter. After years without any except distant glimpses of hunters after game, it would be too much to think that such a hunter might be other than one of the tribe that sent forth those trackers.

There was no chance that the bowman would abandon this prize after wounding it. If the puma continued on its course up the stream, that would bring any pursuers entirely too close to the new home of her people.

⇒7⇐

"We might go and kill that wounded puma and bring the body here to skin out," said Sekto. "If we carried it wrapped in deer hide, that would end the trail the trackers might follow."

"And if they are excellent trackers, they would find where we brushed out our own tracks," said Eketan. Since the battle at the old camp, he seemed more alert than he had been in months. Something about taking up weapons again had roused him from his dreamy state.

"True," Ayina said. "We cannot risk having to kill all these new hunters, as we did those other three. No people would permit another group of their own to disappear without sending many hands of people to search the entire mountain until they found the bodies. Then they would know that we live on the heights and they would not rest until they found and destroyed us."

"Then we must hide again." Teala, ever practical, was already on her feet, gathering up hides for warmth and weapons for food and protection. "We might conceal this house with brush and grass, for it looks like a natural hillock. Then we may come back, when the danger has passed."

A series of nods moved around the circle of people in the dimness of the pit house. Sekto stared hard at Ayina, and she could see that he strained to make her out through his dimming eyes.

"We must go across the water into the stony heights," he said. "This land is too rich, too easy. Any who search will know that if people are here, this is where they will want to live. We must go among the high places where only stone sings to the wind."

It was true, and every person there understood that. No discussion followed the old man's words. Each gathered up a bundle again, and what they decided not to take with them they hid in a deep hole that had been worn by some vanished watercourse running out of the mountainside, far from the glade where their house had been built. They also hid, with stones and sprinkled sand, all trace of digging in the places where they had taken the soil to cover their house.

Then, once more, they crept out of their camp, brushing away any track, straightening any bent twig, any flattened grass behind them. Ayina, coming last, turned to survey the glade; she was relieved to find that the mound forming their house, which was already concealed in the thicket of fir and spruce on the other side of the clearing, seemed as natural a part of the place as the trees that grew there.

Still keeping a close watch on the ground where her people walked, the woman followed Sekto and

Ish-o-tobi, who were just in front of her, toward the
barren heights looming beyond the stream that edged
the forest. The sun turned the peaks gold and red, for
the day had dwindled, and only the topmost heights
still held the sun. Shadows lay long across the land,
once they passed the fringe of trees, and it was hard
to watch where feet stepped.

But the soil was stony, and the small group picked
its way across the ground and waded into the icy
water, which grew deeper and deeper until Sekto had
to carry the child on his skinny shoulders. Then it
was shallower, and Teala, leading as usual, stepped
up and up until she stood, soaked and shivering, in
the breeze at the other side.

"We must stop and dry ourselves or we will be
sick," Ayina said as she dragged her weary feet and
aching legs onto the rocky ground. "Find a place,
Teala, but move along the side of the water, so you
will not drip and leave pockmarks in any dust there
may be farther from the stream. When you locate a
sheltered spot that will conceal a fire, call twice like
a hawk, then once, then once."

Ayina gestured toward the dogs, which were dripping onto the edges of the stream. "Pulap, hide the
places where the dogs have left traces of their passing.
There is no hair between their toes, and if they leave
prints in damp soil, anyone will know the paw marks
are not those of wolves."

She sank onto a ledge of rock, shivering with chill,
while the others huddled close to her to share what
little warmth they possessed. The boy sat on her lap,
and she hugged him to her chest, under her deer-hide
cloak.

Before the sun was entirely off the peaks, the hawk called twice, once, once, and Ayina rose with a sigh of effort. "Now we will go and make fire and cook the venison we brought from the house. Hot food and dry clothing will make us all feel better," she promised.

The place Teala had found was less secure than the old woman had hoped, but it did have a high, curving barrier of boulders, brought down from the height by spring thaws, against which they could build a fire that would be invisible to any on the other side of the water. Dead sticks from the brush beside the stream provided fuel, and there was even dried elk dung to burn.

The fire was small, tightly controlled, but its warmth was cupped in the curve of the stones, and it wasn't long before the Geh-i-nah stopped shivering and Ish-o-tobi's teeth were no longer chattering. The venison, spitted over the coals, began to to sizzle, dripping its scanty juices into the blaze.

Ayina, wrapped in her deer hide while her moccasins and leather apron dried, found herself relaxing. Even if the fire brought enemies, it was worth the risk, for sickness was a far more certain peril than trackers you have never seen and are not even certain are there at all. Her eyes closed, despite her determination to remain awake.

When she opened them again it was to a long howl at no great distance. The dogs were stirring restlessly, but the old men had them in hand.

She moved silently, pulling the deer hide about her more securely, and went out of the shelter of the boulders. The moon was high. The loaf-shaped peak that now loomed above her was silhouetted against the starry sky, the edges picked out in silver by the moonlight.

Again the wolf howled, long and lonely, and from a distance there came a reply. Her expert ear analyzed the sounds, but neither was made by a human throat.

As she turned to resume her place, Netah appeared at her elbow. "Grandmother," she whispered, "is all well?"

"All is very well, Granddaughter," she said. And for the first time in a very long while, Ayina felt that this might be true.

She curled again between Sekto and the child and spread her deer hide over them all. Ish-o-tobi cuddled into the curve of her chest, and she put an arm over his thin shape. Almost before she was settled, she was asleep again.

The rocky height was more distant than it seemed. All day the burdened Geh-i-nah moved through the broken ground toward the base of the greater peak, but their course was so crooked that by the time night came again they had just arrived at their destination.

This was a cleft, slanting away upward into darkness, that cut between the tallest of the peaks and the adjacent one. If there was a possible route by which to reach the top of the stony loaf facing the group, that way should reveal it.

Ayina sent Pulap with the boy to explore the narrow passage. "You are a good climber," she said to the girl, "and the boy is light enough for you to lift if there is a place you cannot reach by climbing. Tomorrow we will all go. If we must climb like lizards up that terrible cliff, then that is what we will do."

She glared at the old men, who looked depressed at the thought of forcing their aged muscles and bones onto the top of the great rock. "Even you, who have learned to wait for death, must go. To find one is as bad as finding us all, and you know that well."

Sekto grunted. "You are right. Cruel, but correct."

Pulap was, of course, well on her way, out of earshot with the boy. Ayina followed her far enough into the ravine to find a spot where another fire could be built. If she and her companions had all been young and strong, she would have done as her people of old had done, camped without fire and without shelter. Given her present family, however, that was inviting sickness and death.

They found a great tangle of fallen rock, up which Pulap scampered. "There is shelter behind this," she called, before returning to help the old men up the uncertain footing and down the other side, which was even more perilous.

Ayina, coming last, heard rattles and rumbles as displaced segments of the rockfall resettled into new conformations. "If anyone comes, we will certainly know," she said aloud; her voice echoed weirdly from the deeps ahead.

Then she realized that the noise of the stones was amplified by the echoes rumbling all around her. It was a fine warning system, she thought.

When she descended carefully on the far side of the debris, she found that the cleft leaned inward above her, almost roofing the deeper reaches of the narrow slot. The pile behind was thick and tall, and any fire they built here would be invisible, for even its gleam against the golden stone of the cliffs would be hidden by the curve around which they had come.

Better still, a draft pulled through the space between the stony heights, and she knew the smoke would rise very high and be dispersed before anyone in the lower country could detect it. She had added to her burden a bundle of sticks. Netah also had carried firewood, for the barren peak promised no fuel.

They built a stingy fire and cooked meat. Pulap and Ish-o-tobi returned, in time, and Ayina fed the child while the girl spoke of their discoveries.

"The cleft curves around this stone mountain, but some distance along its course another cut, a runnel worn by snow runoff, comes down from the height. It runs almost straight up the cliff, but it is narrow enough to brace feet against one side and shoulders against the other. I believe that we may be able to climb that, even Abani and Eketan."

Ayina felt great relief fill her. Given a chance, she knew that her old Geh-i-nah would persist until they inched their way to the top. They had been nurtured in country even steeper than this, and those skills, even in the grip of age and arthritis, would not desert them.

The night was more comfortable than she had thought it might be, for even after the fuel was all burned the rocks they had heated in its coals continued to radiate warmth. The stony barrier deflected the draft, and they were comparatively protected from the chill of the spring night.

When dawn edged up the sky, she was awake, standing on top of the wall of debris, staring back along the curving canyon. She had stripped to a loin-cloth, and her cloak and other equipment were already tightly rolled into a bundle that could be slung across her back.

The others were also awake, and already they had chewed strips of cold venison, made up their burdens, and bound their moccasins tightly onto their feet. Now they took the strips she had cut from the bottom of her own deer hide and wrapped them around their palms, in order to protect them from the painful friction of the rocks they must climb and to give a firmer grip on any handhold they might find.

When they set out, Ish-o-tobi, carrying his own bundle, ran ahead of them like a young goat and stood, at last, beside a dark streak in a narrow area hardly lit at all by the thin line of sky visible above the towering cliffs. When Ayina came up, the others had gathered in a huddle, deciding who should go first.

Before that was decided, Sekto looked down at the dogs about his feet. "What about them?" he asked. "Finding the dogs, dead or alive, is as you said, as bad as finding us."

Ayina closed her eyes. When she opened them, she knew. "The first will take our lengths of cord up with them and when they have reached the top they can let down the line. We will wrap each dog in a fold of hide and they can draw them, one by one, to the top. Then the rest will follow. Now, who should go first?"

"Teala," the child said.

It shocked them all, for they had never thought he might be learning their tongue while they traveled together.

"She is . . . strongest. She can take line. Pull up dogs. Pull up others, if need."

It was an obvious but very intelligent observation for one so young. Ayina nodded with satisfaction. She had made no error in finding this young one and bringing him to her people. He was going to be an asset, whatever happened.

Teala coiled the line, which the old men had twisted in their original camp, forming it of sinew and plant fibers, and put it over one shoulder. Then she planted a foot on a flat slab of rock and sprang upward, catching onto a narrow ledge with both hands. As Ayina watched, the girl worked her way up the chimney, and a patter of grit and small stones rained down on those left below.

The old woman rested, watching, and even as she congratulated herself on coming so far with such aged companions, she heard the eagle cry again, high above the peak. Her heart chilled.

Were those they had fled following them, even now, crossing the stream and coming toward the great pinnacle up which she and the others had to move? But there was nothing else to do, now. They were trapped in this narrow cut, for she could see its end ahead, where the two great stone mountains leaned against each other.

There was no going back.

↘8↙

The sound of Teala as she climbed was reassuring. If any of them could reach the top of this high place it would be her oldest foster grandchild. Ayina kept one ear tuned to the girl's progress and the other to the sounds that might waft up the little canyon from the flatland beyond its mouth.

Ayina, being old but still able, was the obvious one to hold off any attackers who might investigate the cleft in which her people were trapped. No matter how willing the ancient men might be, there was no room for them to wield bow or atlatl in this cramped space. She must go back over the tumble of rockfall and lurk, hidden and attentive, inside the canyon, waiting for anyone who might come.

The two girls, with Ish-o-tobi between them, were staring upward, sheltering their eyes from falling grit with their hands. The boy was listening, his head cocked. The old men were likewise focused upon Teala's progress.

Without speaking, Ayina laid her bundle beside the rock where she had been sitting. She took her knife,

71

her bow, and a clutch of arrows, and slipped backward to the rock pile. Even the small sounds she made in crossing it were lost in the greater noise of Teala's climb, and she gained the other side without the others becoming aware of her leaving.

The sun was high in the east, warming the face of the mountains off to her left. She risked a quick scout beyond the security of the stony slot, lying flat on her belly and moving slowly so as to raise no dust with her motions.

Her ear, laid to the ground, revealed no sound except the grinding of stones in the distant riverbed. Her eyes, still sharp, detected no shapes of men between her and the boulders along the stream's bank. If the searchers were there, they were still hidden in the trees on the other side.

Reassured, she went, lizardlike, back into the shelter of the mountain and retreated beyond the first bend. There she laid out her arrows ready to hand, leaned her lance against the furrowed wall, and knelt, sitting on her heels, her knife in hand, waiting.

Again she heard the call of a hawk in the distance, echoing down the slot in which she sat and bouncing off the faces of the cliffs. To her acute ear it did not sound like the cry of one with feathers, and that kept her alert, though her bones ached and her old knees cried out in pain as she remained still in her ambush.

No sound except that of small creatures came to her, and she found herself leaning against the wall, half dozing. "I am growing too old for this," she admonished herself. "I must remain awake, or all this is for nothing."

She heard a tiny scritch of sound from the rockfall farther into the canyon, then steps so soft that only one whose ears were honed to hear an enemy could have heard them approach. In a moment, Ish-o-tobi rounded the narrow bend and came toward her.

"Teala is up there," the boy whispered. She had to strain to catch his words. "Pulap and Netah are sending the dogs up now. It is time, Grandmother, for you to come."

She sighed. It was one thing to be ready to die for one's family. It was another and much warmer one to continue to live for them. She rose, knees stiff, and helped the boy gather up her weapons.

Together, the two of them returned up the rough way, climbed over the rock pile, and stood again beside the old men. Already Netah was climbing the height, a whimpering dog rising jerkily some man-heights above her as the girl on top pulled him up. As no other dogs remained, Ayina knew that the rest must be on top of the mountain with Teala.

Pulap smiled a welcome. "Grandmother, you must go up just after the men. I will come last. I know how to hide any traces we have left. You are weary, for you have kept watch behind us. Now let me take your place, so that you can rest on top of this mountain."

It was the first time Ayina had ever consented to such a proposal, but her realization, when she found herself almost asleep, made her cautious. She might be careless as well with removing their traces. Pulap knew, for she had taught the girl herself, how to do such things. Best to allow her to finish up in the depths while Ayina climbed.

Sekto went after the boy, as the first of the old men; fixing his gnarled fingers into cracks, finding purchase with his toes, he was steadied by the line that had come back down to aid the elders in their ascent. Then Eketan disappeared up the shadowy height. When Pahket and Abani had gone as well, Ayina turned to Pulap and sighed.

"I have grown old, Granddaughter. It is good to have young hands and young eyes to take my place," she said. Then she turned and went after Abani, ignoring the complaints of her bones and muscles and joints as she climbed.

The line was a blessing, for arthritic fingers sometimes do not grip as tightly as they are told to do. Old knees fail when weight comes down on them as well, and that line kept her from falling more than once. When she emerged into a shallow trough weather-worn into the rocky cliff top, Ayina found herself all but ready to collapse.

Ish-o-tobi was there, with Teala, to pull her the last of the distance. He had her bundle, drawn up with the rest of the supplies before the climbers made the trip, open and her deer hide spread for her to lie on.

She fell onto the thin layer, so weary that the rocky lumps beneath it made no impression on her. About her the old men lay in attitudes of exhaustion; indeed, Sekto and Abani were asleep already, their hearts working visibly in their bony chests with the stress of their labors.

Ayina rolled onto her back and stared up into the sky. The sun was warm at that height, but because of the elevation it was not uncomfortably hot. The sky was a pale blue shell that covered all the land below her position; at one side of that vault an eagle wheeled and at the other a hawk was a tiny shape near the dark line that marked the trees below.

She was too far from the edge to see the area between the height and the stream. When her heart had returned to its usual pace she crawled up beside Teala and stared out over the distances revealed.

Their tiny heads, she knew, could not be detected from below among the ridges and plates of stone that edged the rocky dome. She had observed the edge closely as they approached, judging whether that might not be true, and it was. Even a standing man might be lost in the hugeness of the stony height.

A touch on her leg told her that Pulap had arrived, drawing up the line behind her. "All is well, Grandmother. I have removed any sign that people have been in that canyon. All trace of our fire is hidden beneath slabs of stone, and I found dry wolf dung and placed it carefully to show that wild creatures den there."

Ayina reached to touch her hand. "It is good to have wise children about me," she said. "And it is good to be done with that climb."

"Look!" Teala mouthed, pointing.

Ayina stared along the slender brown finger extended toward the trees beyond the river. A thin curl of smoke rose there, its location hidden by the edge of the forest. So. The hunters still pursued the puma—or the child.

Then, to her horror, she saw the gray-tawny shape of the puma slink free of the low-growing trees along the stream and head directly for the cleft up which her own group had come. Was that its lair? What irony, if they had thought to take refuge in the exact spot to which the animal would lead its hunters.

The creature slipped along, belly close to the ground, visible from the height because its black shadow outlined it. Ayina lay close beside Teala, and the two of them watched intently as the wounded puma made its painful way into the mouth of the cleft. Then they turned to stare at each other, eyes wide.

Ayina turned and wriggled back toward the cluster of resting people. "The enemy is beyond the stream," she said, "and the puma is there in the canyon where we came. The hunters will trail it, for it is surely bleeding from its wounds. We must be silent."

Sekto pushed himself to a sitting position and sighed heavily. "That is strange. But, Ayina, we are well placed. Even if someone among the hunters decides to climb up here, there is only one way to come. We can lie beside that chimney and push them down without even growing weary."

She laughed softly. She'd forgotten, during all those quiet years lower on this range, how quick this man had always been.

"Ish-o-tobi, gather all the throwing stones you can find. There are splits and shards of rock down in the crannies. While they're not comfortable in the hand like those we found in the streams, they will cut painfully if we must fling them at enemies." As she finished, the boy moved away quickly and began piling neat stacks of rocks near the crevice.

Pulap slithered over to peer into the crevice between the leaning mountains, trying to see where the cougar might have taken refuge. "It is too dark down there, and the crack is too narrow where the sides come together," she said. "He may have gone far past the spot where we climbed, as well. There were small openings at the back of the canyon large enough for a cat to crawl into."

Still watching at the edge of the cliff, Teala gave a soft whistle. Ayina and Sekto crept toward her and followed her pointing finger. Five small shapes were crossing the stream, leaping from boulder to boulder. Even as they watched, the last in line missed his step or hit a wet spot on his targeted stone and went flat on his back into the water.

Settling herself as comfortably as possible on the sun-warmed rock, Ayina closed her eyes, knowing that it would take a long time for even those agile men to reach the foot of the mountain on which she lay. "I remember the old times," she said, "when the house of my clan was burned by enemies. I felt much like this, waiting above and watching something that I could do nothing to change."

Sekto sighed. "I, too, remember. But tales are good, when you must wait. Tell us, Ayina, the story of the end of our people's journey, so the young ones may understand."

The others had slipped near, as well, the dogs lying flat on the rock beside the old men, and Ish-o-tobi curling against Eketan's chest. "Tell us, Grandmother!" Netah begged. "We must remember, when we go to our new homes, all the stories of the Geh-i-nah."

So, with plenty of time and little to do, Ayina began, once again, the story of the coming of her people to the canyons of this western country.

❧9❧

Asosaya, the prophet of the Geh-i-nah, was troubled. The People had wandered far, settling in likely spots only to have their lives disrupted by drouth or enemies, which pushed them farther and farther toward the setting sun. For all of her lifetime they had lived on this flat river-meadow, sheltered on the north by a rocky cliff.

The grass was good, and buffalo came into the area often to graze. Water plants growing along the creeks running into the river provided succulent roots, heads that could be eaten like corn, and long, wide leaves for making baskets. The soil layer was thick enough to grow scanty crops of the corn they had brought from the east, but there was something in the ground that caused their bean vines to wither and die.

For the past hand of seasons, Asosaya had watched the weather change, the crops, even enriched with entrails of rabbits and fish, become smaller by the year. This morning she was weaving baskets, despite her crippled arm, while her daughter sat beside her making clay pots.

78

Out on the slope extending to the bluff edging the river the women were digging with their sticks, putting in the seeds for this year's corn. Already the season had turned dry. The spring rains had been stingy, and the river had not risen nearly as high as usual with runoff from the melting snow of the mountains that stood beyond the horizon, many days journey toward the west.

The prophet used her good hand to work the strips of cattail leaf in and out of the ribs formed of its thick stems. The basket seemed to grow naturally between her hands, though because of her bad arm others could do this much more quickly.

"The seeds they plant will not grow," she murmured, keeping her gaze turned toward the distant shapes of the women. "Last season was poor, and we had to gather all the wild plants and seeds we could find to survive it. Even the sunflowers were scarce because of the drouth. Out on the plain beyond the cliff the grass is already withering."

Her daughter, Lakiya, turned her head, gazing into her mother's eyes. She looked surprised, and Asosaya understood that. With two small ones to tend, in addition to her place as the third wife of Toyino, the young woman was too busy to keep a sharp eye on the vagaries of weather and crops.

Asosaya had been widowed for many hands of seasons. She had left the house she had shared with the sister-wives of her dead man to live alone in a small pit house, where she could feel her visions grow inside her. The babble of children and grandchildren was distracting, and for the past few years she had realized that a great prophecy was on its way. She must prepare herself to receive it and to pass it on to her people.

"I have dreamed," she said. That notified any who might hear that this was not a casual thought but a real vision. "I have seen our people thin and starving, and I have seen other hungry people attacking us and driving us away, even from this poor place."

Lakita pummeled the clay, shaping the resulting mass into long rolls, which she began coiling into the form of a pot with a pointed bottom. A carefully shaped depression in the firm soil between her knees contained that point without distorting its shape. The pot grew swiftly upward to the flange at its shoulder, where it turned inward in a graceful curve. She finished the edge with a wet finger, turning back a lip that completed the shape.

When she was done with the basic shape and was ready to smooth the coil marks with a bit of flattened flint, she glanced again at her mother. "Move? The old tales speak of many moves over many lives of our people. Where could we go from here, if such a terrible thing happened? There seem to be enemies in every direction."

Asosaya drew a deep breath as she began weaving into the neck of the basket the remaining lengths of leaf, making a neat pattern of her selvage.

"We go always to the west. We fled the land between the great rivers, if you remember the tales, because of terrible sickness that killed many of the People. We cannot return there, for sickness often waits and strikes again when there is the opportunity.

"No, if we must go, it will be toward those mountains that are also a part of our tales. Men of old traveled there, trying to find a place for their families to rest in peace, but there were others there already, taking up the rich valleys protected by great mountains of stone. And if we must go there, we will be forced to climb into those high forests, where winters are bitterly cold, and to build our homes in places that enemies will find it hard to approach unseen."

Her daughter shivered, and Asosaya felt a chill along her own bones. The thought of uprooting her people yet again from their hard-won security was a frightening one. Yet she knew that she must speak with Iniyoti, who was the eldest and wiser than anyone she knew.

He was so old that he could seldom stir from his fireside. This gave him the time to remember all the history of his clan and his people as a whole. It allowed him to consider the problems brought to him by the Geh-i-nah without haste. His decisions and recommendations were always sensible, though often the young received them with little grace.

Asosaya knew that her vision, coming through Iniyoti, would be heard. Even though she was revered and somewhat feared as prophet of her people, she was timid about making her voice heard among them. For this reason they seldom attended to her words unless they were filtered through the mouth of one of the leaders of the Geh-i-nah.

"I must go to Iniyoti," she said, laying the basket with the others she had made of willow and grass and many other materials found along the streams and out on the prairie land. "He will hear my vision, as he hears everything, without seeming to believe it.

But once he has it in his mind, then something will come of it."

The old man was dreaming in his lodge, which was dug deeply into the rocky soil, its posts the tough small oaks found to the north of the stream. Even in spring, he had a fire, for his ancient bones ached and froze. But he welcomed visitors. Asosaya suspected that was because they brought him new things to think about, and thought was his only activity now.

She scratched at the hide covering his low doorway.

"You are welcome to my house," came the reply.

She stepped inside, nodding to the young woman who sat beyond the fire, weaving fiber bags for gathering the harvest of seeds that would come with summer. "I greet you, Iniyoti," she said.

Old as he was, his eyes were bright in the gleam of the tiny fire. "It is good to see the prophet of the Geh-i-nah," he said in the formal voice that showed he recognized this as more than a casual visit from an old friend.

Timid, as usual, Asosaya slipped down to sit opposite him, sinking back onto her heels. "There has come a vision," she said, without any of the usual niceties that ritual required. "It is not a good one."

Iniyoti stared at her, the red gleam of the fire pricking bright specks into his eyes. His entire body seemed to come alert, for he leaned forward, his head cocked like that of a bird. He had always respected her dreams, once they sank into his consciousness, and now he seemed to expect what she was about to say. She could see that in the grim curve of his lips and the tension in his hands, clenched about the arrow he had been straightening when she entered.

After her rude beginning, the prophet was silent for a long time, her shyness rebuking her. Not for the first time the woman wondered why this gift had been given to her, crippled and timid and reluctant to stand up and speak among her people. It was a burden almost worse than the childhood injury that had left her with a withered arm.

When she spoke, her voice was so quiet that the old man gestured for her to speak up. It was difficult to do, but at last she achieved a tone that he could hear.

"I have dreamed of drouth, Iniyoti. Not the small dry seasons that we have begun to see but a great one lasting for years. I have seen other men, starved and desperate and cruel, coming down upon our village, burning our pit houses, stealing our scanty stores of corn and wild seeds and dried meat. I have seen the great beasts that graze the plains go away to places where the rains still come and grass still grows tall. I have seen our river, here at our feet below its bluff, so dry that one may walk across it without wetting one's sandals."

It all came out in a rush once it began. When the last words were spoken, Asosaya sank back onto her heels, for the urgency of that message had brought her onto her knees. But now the dreadful task was done, and she could go back to weaving baskets, leaving this terrible decision to those who listened to Iniyoti and respected his decisions.

The old man settled back, his hands relaxing to allow both arrow and stone arrow-straightener to drop into his lap. His mouth was set in a grim line, and his eyes

flashed brilliantly in the firelight. For once he seemed
to grasp and believe her words instantly.

"Prophet, you have done well. I will think on this,
and then I will talk with the other elders. Though
we cannot prevent what will come, if we understand
what the future will be that will help us to deal with
it. Thank you, Asosaya."

He nodded permission for her to go, and with great
relief she retreated from the lodge and made her way
back to the spot she shared with her daughter. Materials for her next basket were waiting for her fingers,
and she took up the withes gratefully and began forming the framework for the next one.

The burden of her dream had lightened with the telling. Now it was the burden of decision that awaited,
and she was not the one who must deal with that.

Lakita had shaped the pot beautifully and was using
a sharp bit of flint to mark into it the pattern she had
decided to use. "You have told him?" she asked her
mother.

Asosaya nodded. "He has heard the dream. He has
believed it. The time may be long, but I know that
we will leave this place and go westward yet again.
I had hoped not to see that in my time, though our
tales have always promised that it will happen again."
Tears leaked from the corners of her eyes.

"I fear for my grandchildren," she grieved. "I fear
for the very old and those yet unborn. We have been
born, my daughter, into troubling times. Let us hope
that we will survive to come to a new home in a distant land."

➤10➤

Pain dragged at the puma, now favoring a hind leg and pulling himself forward, moved only by that inner compulsion. He knew that the hunters were behind, but they made little sound.

His nose, less keen than the wolf's, still could detect the rank smell of the fat they had smeared upon themselves. That had roused him more than once, during this flight, when they drew near enough for the breeze to carry their stink to his resting place.

Now he wanted to find a thick clump of bushes and to crawl deep into their shade. He wanted to lie down and close his eyes and let his own body heal or die, whichever might happen. Yet some compulsion drove him forward, his ears flat against his skull, his eyes bright with fever, his fur going scruffy as the wound took its toll of him.

Groaning with effort, the animal moved on, crossing the stream again, now only a brook from which he drank thirstily before climbing onto the grass beyond. There was forest there, and even in his fevered state the animal could detect the taint of ash and the stink of mankind.

He rested for a time against the cool wetness of stone edging a small stream, but he did not sleep and he found that he could not remain there. He was pulled forward by a will stronger than his own, although now he was so weary and confused that he wasn't aware of that.

In time, after the sun set, the puma moved toward the stony peaks that had been his original goal. There was a canyon there with many hiding places. Sheltered by the heights on either side, it should hide him from those he could still sense behind, following his tracks with the persistence of wolves.

Shaking his head, he staggered onward, and in time he found himself entering his old lair. Here, too, there was the smell of intruders, two-legged ones—and as he crept into the hole that had drawn him forward for so many tortured miles, he caught the trace of that small meat that had shared his captivity.

But now the puma was too weary to notice it for more than a moment.

Always the old stories gripped Ayina's listeners. Now, sitting against her shoulder, the boy, who had followed her words with some difficulty, asked, "And did they leave? Where did they go?"

"Ah," Ayina breathed, "that is another tale. And I think that now those hunters may be drawing near enough to be watching, though they could never hear our words from such a distance."

They crept to the edge again and peered downward, their heads sheltered by protrusions of rock and tufts of skimpy growth able to survive even so high and on bare stone. Those who hunted the puma were almost

to the cleft now, and they had sent two of their number ahead to track the beast into the place. The others,
five of them, waited just clear of the boulders rimming
the canyon's mouth.

From the crack along the top of the ravine came
a shrill whistle, carried upward on the draft that
drew through the opening. The afternoon was now
far advanced, and the shadow of the loaf-shaped
mountain enveloped the waiting men as they took
up spears and other implements that Ayina could not
identify from such a height.

The hunters disappeared into the area hidden by the
cliff from the watchers on its top. Then Ayina realized
that they would probably also camp in the shelter of
the slot between the mountains, where the chill wind
of the heights could not reach. There a fire might be
built from, perhaps, some of the very wolf droppings
that her granddaughter had spread.

"We must retain our warmth," she said to her companions. "Gather all the deer hides and the bundle
of furs. The stone will remain warm long into the
night, and we must huddle close together and cover
ourselves with the hides, as if we are the posts of a
pit house. The hides will form its roof."

The wind was already unpleasantly cold, knifing
across the unbroken top of the dome as if to freeze
them where they lay. They found a place where
snowmelt had scored a runnel into the curve of the
rocky top and arranged themselves in a tight circle in
its scanty shelter.

The hides, once in place and held down by sitting
on their lower edges, improved their situation at once.
The knife-edged wind, freshening as the sun set and

the air chilled, was shut away except for tiny currents
that found their way through gaps between the skins.
Their mutual warmth was held inside, and the furs,
arranged about them two by two, helped them gen-
erate enough heat for comfort.

Ayina took a bag of dried meat and seed-bread from
her own bundle and shared the food around. They
settled into noisy munching and crunching, and for
a time nothing was said among the group.

Ish-o-tobi ate hungrily, his shoulder against her side,
his knee against hers, and she smiled in the darkness,
thinking of the starveling she had found. Already she
could see him growing, even after so few days. He
would become a strong man and perhaps one day
he might find a suitable wife. There might be a con-
tinuation of the Geh-i-nah, if young people came into
the tribe.

A thin music crept up from below, finding its way
even under their shelter. A bone flute, she thought.
Then a drum thudded softly, its rhythm throbbing
with that of her pulse.

"They will give us music," she said, chuckling. "We
will have amusement while we wait to see what hap-
pens next."

"I would rather hear more about the People. What
happened after they moved away from the river?"
Netah asked in her breathless voice, though she had
heard the tale as a child and should remember it.

Ayina thought with quiet joy that her people did
care about the old stories, even in the midst of danger. That was good. Though they knew the old tale,
it could comfort them now in this cold, harsh place of
hiding.

"Put away the food that is left," she said, passing the bag so that any crumb might be saved against future hunger. "Then I will tell more of that old time."

The wind rose outside their small and flapping tent of hides. They moved even closer, knees against knees, shoulders against shoulders, and Ish-o-tobi curled into Ayina's lap. She raised her voice to be heard above the whistle of the blast.

It was true. Rain fell less frequently. Grass died to tan dust, and the game that had followed the creeks, which were also dried to mud and puddles, moved away to find better forage. In time, as Asosaya had predicted, other hungry people appeared along the river.

At first, the Geh-i-nah shared their dwindling stores with the few who came. A skinny man, his two emaciated wives, and their dying toddlers were too pitiful to drive away. They ate ravenously, despite the cautioning of the healer woman, and became desperately sick. All except the man died.

That frightened Asosaya, and she went again to Iniyoti. Twisting her fingers together in her lap, she looked down instead of up into those piercing eyes. She was too shy to meet his gaze as she spoke her daring words.

"It is as I have told you, Iniyoti. The famine has begun, and the first of those people have arrived."

He shook his grizzled head. "Only one survives, hardly enough to make a difference. It will rain, in time, and the grass will turn green again. The cattails will thrust up through the mud and provide food, even if it is too late for the corn to grow. We will survive this, as we have other drouths since our people came here."

Stubbornly, the prophet shook her head in turn. "No. I have dreamed again. This drouth will not go away in a hand of seasons. It will endure for a long, long time. I see the river with dust in its bed. I see the plain turned brown and dusty, with devil winds swirling down its length."

She drew a deep breath, and her voice was clear as she said, "I see our village empty, with only holes where posts were sunk to mark where our houses now stand." She looked up, feeling her face hot with embarrassment.

"Iniyoti, I see strangers walking where we sit, staggering with hunger and thirst and digging in the riverbed in vain for water to drink. We must go, or we will die."

Never had the prophet spoken so strongly to anyone. Even her own daughters had not heard her voice rise or seen her eyes flash with the intensity of her feeling. Iniyoti stared at her for a moment, his mouth open with astonishment.

"I will speak to the elders," he said at last. "But you must speak to them as well. Unless they hear your voice, see your face, they will do as I have done. They will wait until it is too late. Come with me, Asosaya. We must take counsel with our peers."

Never before had she thought of herself as the equal of those elders. Pili the healer was revered by all the People. Kostiyo the priest held the ears of the gods of wind and sun and soil, and it was through him that the people made certain their crops would grow. He had become haggard and grim these past moons, as he saw his efforts achieve nothing.

Umforta the fighter knew how to protect his people from their infrequent enemies and from predators that sometimes threatened them. He was tall, though stooped with age, and the young men listened to him with attentive faces, absorbing all his accumulated skill.

No, she had not thought a prophet to be the peer of any of these, but here she stood in the lodge of Pili, amid the circle of elders. They looked at her solemnly, and she realized with sudden clarity that they were waiting for her to give them information that would allow them to make this terrible decision.

So she spoke again, this time standing straight, her gaze fixed on the joining of the posts at the peak of the domed roof. The importance of her message filled her, and she forgot her fear of being noticed as she spoke. When she fell silent, the others were also quiet for many heartbeats.

"It is as we feared," said Pili. "When I saw the women and the children die, among those who came down the river, I had a bad feeling in my heart. The man who is left alive has learned some of our words, and he speaks of starvation, of dead beasts lying on the plain, of forests with withered leaves in the mountains beyond the river to north and east."

Umforta grunted. "If that is true, we must not go north, for that will give us no help. We should send runners westward, to find if there is yet water there, forests with game, and wild plants that will sustain us through the winter."

Iniyoti nodded agreement. "We cannot move the entire village without knowing that we are going in the right direction. Choose three men, Umforta. Send them west, toward the mountains that our scouts found in the time of our grandfathers, before we settled in this place.

"We have stores set aside for times of drouth and hunger. We can wait until they return and still have enough food to keep us alive in that new place until we can plant and harvest crops and hunt for meat in the high places."

Asosaya sat back from the fire in the middle of the lodge, watching, listening. She had done her duty, spoken amid her people, and now she was shaking with delayed reaction. Surely there was time to find a refuge for the Geh-i-nah, there in those distant mountains!

Wind-driven dust stung the eyes and filled the nostrils. Cracked mud floored the riverbed, and the creeks were only hard-edged grooves in the land. The willows turned yellow and shed their leaves, and the cottonwoods also withered. Asosaya huddled her bad arm to her chest and rocked back and forth in the shade of the lodge, grieving for the land that had nourished her people for so long.

Lakita was inside, feeding her youngest. The child was fretful and cried much now because the dust was harder on tiny ones than on their elders.

Among the People it was a time of waiting, while the three young men, the strongest runners, the best nourished of those left in the families, made their journey. Asosaya longed for their return. Many had become sick, others had died since the scouts left. Time was dwindling with the numbers of the People.

She was not one of those who knew where to find herbs and seeds and other valuable foodstuffs. Her gift, aside from weaving baskets, was that of dreaming truly of the future, and now that was used up and she felt that she was only a burden upon her family.

The food she ate could nourish the grandchildren and her daughters. The journey they must make when the men returned would try even the strongest, and Asosaya had never been strong. That crippled arm seemed to drag at her shoulder, wearying her back and making even her legs falter.

No, she was useless. It was time she left the village, stopped taking her share from the stores of food, and went out to meet her ancestors, who might welcome even her into the Other Place.

Lakita was still inside the lodge, though the baby had quieted. No one was in sight as the woman, who was not old but had never really been young, rose unsteadily, settled her deer-hide cloak about her shoulders and over her head to keep off the blown dust, and set out upriver.

No children played outdoors, for they had little energy. No woman scraped hopelessly at the place where the corn had been planted, for not even stubble remained there. She knew that there was no one to see her as she tottered away into the wind to the place where the bison used to come down to the river to drink. There she could climb up the cliff onto the prairie and walk away.

Once she achieved that, she stood staring about her. She had not walked so far since the drouth began; nothing had prepared her for the look of the land that once had been lush with buffalo grass higher than the head of a man. Now the dun-colored plain merged with the dust-colored sky at the edge of seeing.

The wind stirred nothing but grit, for no grass was left except stiff stubble that only quivered in the gusts. Its scritching frictions sounded like the warning of a rattlesnake, though even snakes had become scarce as the villagers hunted them down and dried their meat for the coming journey.

Asosaya sighed and coughed, for grit choked her. This was not going to be an easy departure from the world, she could see. Hunger, thirst, abrasion, exhaustion—she understood the things that would torture her before she died.

Yet the woman understood even more clearly the importance of preserving the lives of the young. She must go, as many of the very old had already done, in order to allow the children to live. If the Geh-i-nah were to go forward into another life among the mountains, there must be young ones to carry forward their blood.

She staggered as a particularly hard gust caught her, almost toppling her unsteady balance. Then she realized that she need not walk away from the wind. Now that she was above the river canyon she could turn westward, so the blast was not at her back but side-on, easier to endure without falling.

Holding the robe over her face, she moved onward, her feet fumbling over the uneven ground but keeping on their way with grim determination. When the hands caught her elbows, turning her toward the invisible person who held her, Asosaya's heart almost stopped with shock.

The robe slid from her face, and she looked into the eyes of Pemayo, one of the runners sent west. "What are you doing here?" he demanded, before he recognized her.

"I am going to the Other Place," she replied calmly. "If the young are to travel and survive once they arrive, those of us who are of no worth must leave now. But before I go—did you find a place where the People can live? A place with grass and forest and game?"

He gazed into her eyes, his expression carefully controlled, though his sadness showed in his eyes. "There are great mountains there, and when you travel far enough they are rich with running waters and forests of pines and aspens and firs. Deer and elk and other animals thrive there, and when you can find pockets of soil it seems rich enough to grow corn and beans and squash." His young voice almost broke.

He cleared his throat and spoke again. "We can live there, Asosaya. Remember that as you go to the Other Place. Tell our ancestors, when you meet them there, that you have helped to save our People."

She managed to smile, though her heart was skipping treacherously and her limbs felt weak and unreliable. "Go quickly, Pemayo. Tell the Geh-i-nah." She turned away from him, pulling her robe about her nose and mouth.

The wind pushed her; the dust swirled about her. Asosaya, the prophet of her People, went away into the barren prairie and did not return.

❧11❧

The child in Ayina's lap gave a short sob, as if the sadness of the story had caught at him painfully. The others, familiar with this story heard long years in the past, still seemed to hold their breaths as they thought of that terrible time in the history of their people.

The distant music from the hunters camped below had long since died away, and Ayina shifted her cramped limbs, setting the boy beside her. "It is time to sleep. We must wake early and keep close watch on those below. We cannot guess what the cat will do or how its hunters will behave."

The Geh-i-nah settled as best they could on the thin skins beneath them, laying body to body to conserve heat on that unprotected height. With the boy's sharp shoulder digging into her chest, Ayina curled herself into a ball, feeling at her back the skinny frame of Sekto and at her feet one of the quiet dogs. That was a comfort, for the beast was warming her chilled feet with its thin body.

She sank into darkness, stilling her mind, controlling her tendency to start when the dog jerked against her, dreaming of a dash after a rabbit or a woodchuck. When she slept, it was with her senses triggered for any sound that might mean danger, though she knew that Pulap had taken the first watch. The young woman had her head out of the skin tent, listening to the night.

Ayina woke before dawn, for the wind died to a murmur, and the softening of its whistling roused her from a dream of running through stony heights, pursued by faceless hunters. Ish-o-tobi had moved in his sleep, leaving her on her back, her elbow against Sekto, her feet burrowed into the mangy coat of the dog.

Before she opened her eyes, Ayina listened intently to the predawn stillness. In the distance some predator howled, but otherwise only the faint hiss of breeze on stone reached her ears. The regular breathing of her companions was so familiar that she did not hear it at all, unless one of the old men snorted or groaned.

A foot moved to find hers and gave three gentle nudges. That must be the granddaughter who was on watch, Ayina knew. Some sound or change in the feel of the night must have caught her attention. Carefully, the woman eased herself out of her cramped position and slipped from under the tented hides.

Standing erect on the barren height, she surveyed the surrounding sky. A faint line of light now marked the east, though as yet no wash of visibility touched the face of the adjacent mountain.

The cranny that was the canyon etched a black line on the pale stone beyond the runnel where they had camped. Ayina moved on silent sandals to its edge. Lying flat, she inched her eyes over the verge and stared down.

No glimmer of coals from a dying fire interrupted the darkness in those deeps. She heard, however, a scritching and a scratching sound that was not that of any human being. Carried along the confines of the enclosed canyon, that faint noise told her something was moving down there—or up onto the dome of rock where she stood?

Ayina's heart thudded one great beat of fear. Was that trapped puma climbing by some unknown route to the security of the mountaintop? If that were so, then surely its hunters would find traces, for its claws must certainly mark the way it came. And that would lead those strangers directly to the refuge of her people.

She turned toward the dim patch that was the shelter. "Netah?" she whispered. "Did you hear a strange sound from below?"

The girl crawled out and wrapped a deer hide about her shoulders. She leaned until her face was very near before saying, "Yes, Grandmother. It sounds like something climbing. Not a man. The puma?"

Now the line of light had grown broader, and Netah's face was a blur in the tenuous dawn. Her eyes were wide, her tender mouth uncharacteristically grim as she faced Ayina.

"If so, we must deal with it," the old woman said. "Wake the others. Quietly. I will watch while you give them meat from my bag and water from the skin. Then we must arm ourselves and wait for what may come."

The sky was paling now, and below, the land was turning into a patchwork of grays and blacks. The sounds from the canyon, still soft and persistent, were nearer and more distinct as Ayina turned to her people.

"Arm yourselves. Sekto, you and Pahket take arrows and bow and atlatl and stand back at some distance. There is room to use those weapons, if need be. Eketan, here is your spear. Abani, your club should serve you well." She knew she need not instruct her granddaughters. They understood what must be done if the big cat emerged onto the mountaintop.

They crouched patiently on their heels, holding weapons at convenient angles. Ayina was relaxed, resting even as she waited. They knew, the Geh-i-nah, how to accept what came without stress; now as the sun rose above the lower country, smoothing warm fingers of gold against the faces of the cliffs, she knew that her companions were silently bidding farewell to earth and sky, in case things should not go well.

Death was of no concern. It was living that demanded the utmost of a person and a tribe. It was enduring the rigors of existence that was difficult. Dying was easy.

With sudden vigor, she rose to her full height and brought up her spear. Down the canyon, where the crack was narrowest, a dark body heaved itself onto the top of the dome. It was, indeed, the puma, its hide dappled with dried blood, its sides heaving with exertion.

In the canyon there was now the sound of men moving, talking, climbing. Ayina gestured for her people to move, circling beyond the animal, which now lay flat, ears back, eyes blazing as the dogs growled softly in their throats. Sekto controlled them, and they held their places, but the cat was obviously not going to move as long as they confronted it.

Ish-o-tobi, at a gesture from Ayina, darted back, grabbing two dogs by the scruff of the neck as he passed. The Geh-i-nah eased backward as well, for Ayina realized that this weary animal was the weapon they needed against those hunters who were climbing the cliffs toward her people.

"There," she whispered, pointing. The three girls moved toward the other side of the beast, gently, slowly, trying not to frighten it more than it was already. As they crept onward, the animal moved up the crack, and Ayina backed away in her own turn.

"There," she said again, her voice barely audible.

Now her people saw the plan. She had marked the spot toward which they should drive the puma, and now they pushed the battered animal toward it. It growled, backing reluctantly toward the treacherous edge of the cliff it had climbed with such pain and effort.

"Now!" Ayina leaped toward the puma, her spear goading it toward the drop, and behind her came the others, silent but relentless, their weapons ready.

The puma gave a despairing shriek and leaped into the cleft. Below there was a chorus of yells and grunts, as their intended prey descended unexpectedly onto the heads of its hunters. The sound of a desperate struggle grated and groaned below, but Ayina did not wait to learn the end of the engagement.

She caught up all she could carry of their supplies and led her laden people across the great sweep of the mountaintop, their sandals and moccasins quiet on the stone as they ran. At last they reached the steep cliff that edged its southern side, where she dropped onto her knees, panting as desperately as the puma had done.

The girls gathered hides and bundles together while she caught her breath and recovered something of her strength. "Will we go down here?" asked Teala.

Ayina nodded. It was the only way. If any of the hunters survived in condition to continue their climb, the Geh-i-nah must be gone from that height as if they had never existed. At her gesture, the bundles were dropped over the edge, catching the steep slope beneath and gliding down and out of sight in the detritus below.

Teala was securing the line to a spur of rock. Already Ish-o-tobi had one of the wary dogs in place, and Netah was securing the rope about his stiff and resentful body.

He gave a doleful yip as he was pushed over the edge, but the cord held fast and the girls let him down until his paws could scrabble against the gentler curve of the slope far beneath them. The others followed quickly and stood, claws slipping among the scree, gazing upward at the people who now began descending the cliff.

Ayina sent the old men next, for the strongest backs were needed to control that long descent. The line was fraying, as well, and she watched it anxiously until the last, Eketan, was beside his peers.

Now the dogs moved away, clattering and sniffing among the slabs of stone and litter of rocks that slanted away in a fan toward the scrub-grown country at its edge. Abani and Eketan followed them, their feet cautious among the treacherous layers.

Sekto and Pulap stood waiting for Ish-o-tobi to reach their hands. Ayina went next, staring up, at every swing of the line, at the girls who were lowering her.

Teala, oldest and wisest of the young women, came last, after detaching the cord from its spur and wrapping it about her waist. Her clever fingers seemed to find holds where none could be seen, and her toes edged into crannies invisible to those below her. Ayina felt her heart pain her as she suffered that long descent with her granddaughter.

But at last they were all down, and the sun was overhead, hiding them in the shadows of the overhang beneath which they sheltered to rest. Even if the hunters came to peer over the edge of this particular cliff, they would not see anything amiss, Ayina hoped.

The dogs, cowed by the unusual events of the past days, lay flat underfoot. Not even a sniff or a growl came from their flea-ridden huddle.

As Ayina lay on her robe beneath an angle formed by a half-fallen slab and a pine tree, she closed her eyes and thought of how easily this day might have gone differently. The hunters might have followed more closely after their prey. The puma might have retained more strength with which to attack its tormentors on top of the mountain.

Worst of all, their fragile rope might have broken under the repeated stresses they had demanded of it. Before anything else, once they were clear of those strangers, they must kill deer and twist another stout rope of hide and tendon and dog hair.

Then, exhausted with exertion and worry, Ayina fell asleep, and this time she did not dream at all.

≫12≪

They rested, but only for a short while. The hunters were still too near, and there was no way to know what damage the puma might have done to its pursuers. If those were men of determination, they might well leave their injured to nurse their wounds. If the puma had escaped, they would send the fit hunters after their quarry.

As they moved into the rough country beyond the cliff, Ayina wondered if her people could manage both to escape these strangers and find their way to the meeting place with the Ahye-tum-datsehe. She feared that the young men who would become husbands of her granddaughters might come to the meeting place, only to find that their brides never arrived.

Ish-o-tobi walked ahead of her, two of the dogs flanking him. She realized that the boy was now able to understand her language, although it seemed too soon for anyone so young to learn a tongue unlike his own. Yet he seemed to comprehend most of what was said to him and was even able to form sentences when he needed to speak.

Perhaps, she thought, he might know something about those hunters and could now explain something of his own predicament that had sent him fleeing to his encounter with the Geh-i-nah.

"Tobi," she said, picking her way along a dry runnel lined with flat-edged stones and water-rounded cobbles, "why were you running from those men?"

His thin back stiffened for an instant. Then he relaxed and turned his head to stare into her eyes. After searching her face thoroughly, he looked down again, choosing his steps and his words with equal care.

His small voice floated back to her as he went. "I not that people. I from other place where is mountain. They come to hunt, you see? I go out to find wood for fire. They catch me, carry me back like wapiti they have kill, tie onto stick. They cook wapiti. They beat me, put me in small lodge made of poles, when they come to village. There in bigger lodge they keep a puma, right beside.

"I hear talk. They talk some like me, and I hear they send me to the god. I no want to go with fire and knife, so I bite free and run. Then you find. But they want me for god, or they not follow so long."

Ayina had thought that must be the case. But she had another question, though she doubted if the boy would know the answer.

"Why are they hunting that puma? Is that the same one they had in the village? It seems that tracking it is keeping them from trying to find you, if they're so anxious to take you back."

Now Ish-o-tobi halted. They were at the end of the line of walkers, and the back of Eketan disappeared in a tangle of brush as he turned to face her. "They say sacrifice cat, too. Puma sacred to them. I go to the gods, they wrap me in his fur, still warm from his blood."

So there it was. Ayina snorted with revulsion. Death was her enemy, as it was the enemy of all healers. At its best, life here in the mountains was dangerous enough without killing any who need not die. She had slain those who approached her village, back there on the other side of the mountain, but that had been in the interest of survival.

Taking a child for the sole purpose of killing him was a dreadful thing, and she spat at the thought. What kind of people were those hunters from the lower country?

She nodded toward the sound of diminishing footsteps, and the boy turned obediently and hurried after the group. Ayina, at the end of the file, watched for broken twigs or careless scrapes from foot or weapon that might betray their route to any who followed. She had no desire to fall into the hands of the killers of children.

It was very dark in the canyon they chose as their course, for the sun was down behind the farther peaks. Teala, leading the band, kindled a torch, for the footing was treacherous.

Ayina was trudging alone, still watchful, though exhaustion dimmed her vision. To her relief, there was forest along the bottom of the canyon, which promised fuel for a good fire when they stopped at last.

When Teala signaled with her torch, those who followed her came gladly to drop onto the ground about her. She looked down at Ayina. "I will find a hidden nook where we can build our fire," she said. "We must eat hot meat, for this day has tried us all. The woodchucks Netah killed along the way will feed us well."

Ayina nodded, the pain in her legs now so severe that she did not dare speak for fear of crying out. All the control that she had so painfully learned in her life was required to keep her face smooth and her voice even when she spoke at last.

"It may be that those men follow us still. Find a secure place, Teala, where our fire will be sheltered and its smoke will not betray us." Then she sank with her back to a boulder and closed her eyes. She was getting entirely too old for such exertions.

She dozed unexpectedly, even her innate caution overcome by weariness. A touch at her shoulder roused her to see Teala's concerned face, lit by a flickering torch, bending above her.

"Come, Grandmother. I have found a good place. We may rest there without danger, I believe," the girl said. She tugged Ayina's proffered hand, helping her rise, and the two of them moved along the rough bottom of the canyon toward complete darkness.

That turned out to be a huge barrier of stone that thrust out into the narrow passage, leaving only a slit through which to enter the space beyond. The rock was black, seeming to absorb the feeble torchlight; once they were past its bulk they found themselves in an area half roofed by slabs that had fallen forward from the left-hand cliffs, only to come to rest against the wall opposite.

The floor of this sheltered place was littered with shards of rock, but Ish-o-tobi, weary as he must be, was sweeping away the debris to make a place for his elders to sleep. Pulap was squatting over a neat cone of dry branches that she must have gathered as they came through the trees along the canyon.

In a moment Teala thrust her torch against its base, and the pile kindled. Netah was skinning the wood-chucks, which had been gutted as soon as she killed them to prevent their meat from spoiling. She peeled the fur from the plump bodies and laid each neatly aside to be stretched on frames and carried along. Who knew when one of their number would need a bit of fur for a cap or for patching?

When the four carcasses were spitted over the fire, the group collapsed onto their unrolled hide blankets and rested. Ayina felt her gut growl with hunger, for even with their exertions they had eaten little along the way. It was not the habit of the Geh-i-nah to eat more often than once a day, in ordinary times, but she determined that as long as they were moving so fast and so far they must save back cooked food from the nightly meal so as to have something to chew as they traveled.

When most of the meat was transferred to their lean bellies, she gathered up the scraps along with bones containing marrow and put them into her food bag. There she had been putting occasional edibles she'd found as she traveled, and now several kinds of berries jostled leaves of healing herbs, withered but still usable.

They were still very high, and the night was chilly. Ish-o-tobi nestled against her as she lay on her blanket and the others settled down after banking the fire with dirt and grit from the ground. "Tell more. About people who leave," the boy's small voice said to the darkness.

Ayina almost groaned, for she was so tired she hardly remembered the old tale herself. Yet she knew that no one would sleep for some time, until their muscles relaxed and their minds stopped fluttering like the leaves of the cottonwood tree. A story would ease them into rest, and she began. . . .

"So they went away from that river that had been so kind to them. Grieving for Asosaya and the people who had died, they followed the scout back toward the mountains where he had left his fellows to locate a good place for their people. . . ."

Hanonit felt very young and unsure. He was surprised to find himself chosen as one of the scouts, though later he had realized that he was almost the strongest of the young men remaining to the Geh-i-nah. Yet now he was given the task of locating a site for the new village, and he understood that this was a very serious matter.

Kesotat, his remaining companion, was older, and he had taken for himself the task of finding game trails and patches of edible plants. As one of the healer's sons, he understood that sort of work better than did Hanonit.

Now the younger boy moved almost aimlessly along the foot of a shaggy mountain, finding and discarding, for one reason or another, various streams that might be water supplies. He needed a relatively flat space large enough to hold the pit houses that his people would build here. It should be on the sheltered side of the height against which it lay, and there should be water near, but not so near that it might lead enemies to the village.

That sounded simple, but he found that such a place seemed not to exist. He found flat places of the right size, yet so distant from water that it would be difficult to supply the People's needs. Others were sheltered from the winter winds but were too small.

On and on he wandered, searching. Above him loomed a peak with clouds about its head. The trees were large firs interspersed with aspen, and under their branches grew serviceberry bushes and small oaks that would bear acorns for meal, which he noted with satisfaction. Hearing the gurgle of water, he rounded a mossy boulder to find beyond it the place for which he had been seeking.

It was spread like a great, needle-strewn blanket between a sheer wall of rosy stone and a considerable cliff that dropped straight for many man-heights. It would be easy to defend, he saw at once, for only from the other side could an enemy possibly approach with any ease.

He peered up through the dark-needled branches to check the sun. Yes, the wall was to the northwest, a bastion against blizzards, while the cliff was to the southeast. The boulder protected the approach from the east. He headed across the space to see what might lie around the belly of the mountain on that westward side.

Much to his surprise, he found a steep ravine, lined with ferns and moisture-laden plants, running down from the height beyond the knee of the mountain. He heard from below the water sound that had brought him here. Hanonit suspected that someplace far below that brook might run into a larger one—perhaps even a river. From the sound, even this was a considerable stream.

He turned to look again at the place he had found. It was protected from the north winds and the snows that would surely be heavy here so high in the mountains. It had water near but not too near, and it was invisible from the bed of the stream. It was defensible. And it was large enough to contain not only the number of houses that had formed their old village but to provide space for others, if the numbers of the Geh-i-nah should grow.

The boy marked the place well in his mind, recalling the shape of the peak that topped this mountain, the intricate set of game trails he had followed to arrive here, the direction of the canyon below. He knew he would not lose it, for his people trained their memories to lose nothing.

≫13≪

The child squirmed against Ayina, sighing. "He find good place."

"A very good place, in these mountains where we used to hide, though it took a long while for the People to come there. For they were thin and weary and autumn came before they arrived. Many wanted to stop in the river valleys they found, once they traveled out of the area where the drouth held sway."

If Iniyoti had not died, Pili thought, it would have been much easier to move their suffering people westward. But the old man, feeble enough before the hard times came upon them, had not long survived the loss of Asosaya. More than anyone had realized, the elder had relied upon her prophecies to help guide his people, and when she walked away, unseen, into the wind she seemed to take his strength with her.

That left only Umforta, who, though strong, was never particularly wise, and Kostiyo to help her advise and nag and bully their people into motion. The priest was wise in the ways of the gods, but Pili had found over her long life that this did not often help in dealing with humankind.

So she shook her aching bones into motion and became the harsh mother-in-law of the village. The young mothers stared at her, shocked to see the gentle healer of their children turn so stern and cruel. But she managed to harry them into motion at last, using Umforta's strong back to good advantage and Kostiyo's threats of the anger of the gods to somewhat less effect.

Among the three, they urged the uprooted village along the river until it turned away from their course. Its scanty water had been a source of comfort for everyone, and when they filled gourds and waterskins and moved into the dry country many wailed and tried to turn back.

But Pili was no weakling to be persuaded by tears. She drove her people before her, beating those who hung back and berating those who complained until all trudged forward in silence, following the travois-laden dogs. Sullenly the remaining old men and women, the young mothers and fathers herded the children, carried the babies who survived, and stared into the west, where as yet no notch against the sky promised refuge in the mountains.

It was a terrible journey, requiring many weeks. When at last they staggered down into a river valley, where green grass was dotted with grazing elk and bison, the people planted their feet and refused to go on.

Pili knew that this rich country was already tenanted. Traces of old campfires and piles of bones showed where hunters had made their camps over many generations. Patches of chippings told her that these people had shaped arrows here for many, many seasons as well.

"We will be attacked if we build our houses here," she told her daughters, but they shook their heads, their gazes fixed on the few children who remained to them.

Tanoma pointed to her son. "If he is to live, we must stop and make our homes. These weeks of travel have thinned the children to bones; they cannot survive another journey."

"Will they survive spears and arrows?" Pili asked, her voice rising with impatience. "Do you want to find a place where there is safety, or do you just want to stop? We might rest here for a time, but if we begin setting posts and digging pits for our houses, I am certain that those who live in this country will see it as a wrong and will come upon us to drive us out."

But even Kostiyo did not believe her, though Umforta listened uncomfortably and made blustering comments about the strength of their own warriors. "Warriors?" the healer asked. "Where are they? I see four double hands of men, some mere boys, some so old they can hardly lift their spears. I see women who are weakened with hunger and long travel. Even among those who can still lift their spears, most have been sick, as well.

"Who knows how many strangers may attack us? It is certain they will be stronger than we, for you can see from the grass and the game that they have not been stricken by the drouth we faced in the east. They will be vigorous and full of life, while we are worn and weary."

She could not make them understand, and at last she gave up and sat in her hide shelter, allowing them to begin digging out the pits for houses. Every evening she prayed to the setting sun that it would rise again on a living village, but she had no faith that her prayer would be answered.

Before they had done more than dig the post holes for the first house, a rain of arrows pelted down among them as they rose to build their morning fires. Six fell at once before Pili's eyes.

Ignoring the screams of both attackers and attacked, Pili crept from her hide shelter and went to tend the injured. Ducking and swerving to make herself a smaller target, she moved to the first of the wounded. It was her own daughter, Tanoma, and she was dead.

Pili dammed up the river of tears and lamentations that threatened to overcome her. There was no time for feelings now. There was work to be done if any were to survive this foolish endeavor.

As she darted to the next downed figure, Umforta thundered past, his bow twanging, for he aimed and loosed arrows on the move. It was one thing he did well, she admitted to herself, and this was certainly the correct time to use such skills. If she did not have to tend the wounded she might pick up a spear and do some damage to their enemies herself.

The rest of the men and the skilled women, young and old, sick and well, knew what to do. They slid into the morning mist, armed with hastily gathered spears, bows, arrows and atlatl, and before she had reached the last of the wounded she heard sounds of battle in the thick growths of willows and cottonwoods along the river.

Shouts of victory in an alien tongue turned to screams. Crashing and thrashing among the growth beside the stream told her that bitter struggles took place there. From time to time an arrow sang over her head, very near and yet by some happy chance missing her entirely.

Nothing distracted her from her work. By the time the bedraggled remnant of her people's defenders returned, having driven off the strangers, she had moved every victim into shelter and bound up the worst of their wounds.

The mothers and children were working steadily, seeing what must be done; fires were kindled already, pots boiling beside them as the children watched heating stones, lifted them with wooden tongs, and dropped them into the water. There would be need for herbal teas and steaming masses of plantain to heal the raw wounds of their people.

Umforta came to kneel beside Pili, who had time at last to straighten her daughter's limbs and to keen a mourning song over her still body. "They are gone, Pili," he said.

He touched Tanoma's glossy hair with one finger, looking strangely sad for a warrior. "We remained here too long. You were right—the people who belong here will attack and attack until we leave. So we must leave at once."

She looked up into his eyes, her bitterness touching her tongue. "Indeed, Umforta. Where are all those strong warriors you bragged about before this happened? Now we must run like whipped curs, fleeing blindly until we come to the mountains."

He stared down at Tanoma, his finger still stroking her hair. "The wounded must be moved. We are making carriers, using the willow poles from beside the river, for we must go before the sun sets, if our attackers do not return. When they come again, we must be well on our way."

Pili felt a dim pity for the big man, so simple and so filled with grief. She managed to rise from her daughter's side. "And the dead? Is there time to make the death fires for them?"

He looked shocked. "We would not leave our dead to wander always, shut away from the Other Place. Even for Asosaya, who went and was never seen again, the chants were sung and the rituals performed, so that her spirit would find ease. Prepare your daughter, Pili. We will ready the four others who died among the cottonwoods. But once the fires are lighted for them, we must hurry away."

She knew he was right. The smoke would bring back those enemies, but once they saw the burning bodies they would not, she felt certain, disturb the flames. All people were wary of the dead.

As Pili followed the young scout who had come to take them to refuge, she deliberately forced herself to face only forward. To look back at the place where the smoke of her daughter's burning flesh mingled with that of four of her people would weaken her. She could not afford that, for this journey was aging her beyond her years.

So she set her gaze upon Pemayo's back and made her feet continue forward, stepping in his tracks. She could hear the tread of many pairs of sandals and skin shoes following. Without looking, she knew that the two wounded, incapable of walking, were borne just behind her, so that she would be at hand if they needed her healing arts.

Pili watched the line of low trees that marked the course of the river canyon, off to the right and ahead of the column of marching Geh-i-nah. As if reading her thought, Pemayo said, "We will keep that in view for a long while, but we will turn southward to avoid the green valley where it runs out of the mountains. Fierce people live there. They almost caught the three of us as we traveled westward."

"So the easy country is already occupied," she murmured to his dusky back, which was wrapped in a deer hide against the chill that came with evening. "It is not surprising, given the many kinds we and our ancestors have seen as we came from the Great River many generations ago. The land is thick with people, and none welcome intruders."

They went until they could move no more. The watchers who guarded their rear came in at last with the word that there was no sign of pursuit. The exhausted band camped, fireless, and chewed what dried meat they had brought. Then they slept, flinging themselves down on their blankets, regardless of the chill of this high country.

Pili could not sleep.

Her heart was with her daughter, rising like smoke after the spirit of Tanoma as she rode the chanted hymns toward the Other Place. The moans of the wounded might move her body to tend them, from time to time, but the heart of Pili the healer went into death with her child.

If their earlier travels had been hard, they were insignificant compared with those to come. Abrupt cones of mountains thrust up at the edge of seeing in the long swells of dry grassland. Once the Geh-i-nah passed the smaller ones in the east, larger ones came into view.

Buttes striped with pink and ocher, white and brown rose about them, some wearing spills of snowy sand trickling from high layers where some recent storm had washed it down the sloping faces of the cliffs. There was water in creeks and occasional small rivers, but the terrain was terrible for such weary people to cover.

They found they must avoid the inhabited river valleys, keeping to what smaller streams they could find. When they moved into a jumble of mountains among which the meadows were rich but too small to hold enough game or to grow enough corn to support many people, they found, at last, no potential enemies. That was a relief to their burdened minds.

They followed a rock-lined stream whose banks were fringed with narrow green bands of growth flanked by harsh desert. On they went, day after terrible day, toward mountains looming ahead that must be avoided or crossed.

At last they came to a place where a sheer wall of fluted golden stone rose beyond the flatter area they had just crossed. The cliffs rose to the sky, Pili thought, staring up in stunned despair at the terrible climb they must make.

"If we follow the river at the foot of that cliff, no matter how far out of our way it might lead us, can we avoid climbing it?" she asked the youngster.

"We tried that," he said, "along its course. But it is deep and swift and it is cut straight down between sheer heights. Unless you could follow it by wading in its bed, and that is impossible, it is useless. We must climb. But the three of us climbed it before and came to no hurt."

Pili sighed, but she knew her people. They had come across all these terrible lands already. They were capable of going farther if they must.

They rested for two days beside the cold depths of the river. Umforta, being older and wiser than the three scouts, searched upstream and down until he found a spot where a wide stretch of stone had fallen from the face of the cliff into the stream, narrowing the channel, leaving great chunks and slabs almost across the width of the stream.

When he came for Pili, she followed him to the place and nodded. "You have saved lives, Umforta," she told the warrior. "We can cut small trees and tie them together with lines. The strongest of us all, who must be Pemayo, I think, can take a line across to the first boulder. Then we can make a barrier that will keep the weaker people from being swept away or battered against the rocks. This is a good place."

The old man beamed. She knew he had been full of grief since the disaster in that lush valley, and now he had redeemed himself in his own eyes. That was good. People at ease with themselves were stronger and more useful than were those who were filled with self-doubt and sorrow.

They crossed early in the morning, while somewhere much farther up the river's course a part of
the water was locked in early-morning ice. Drenched,
soaked, filled with dread, Pili came last, after the
wounded had been handed along a chain of hands,
and set her foot at the base of that terrible precipice.
Tomorrow she must force her old bones up that wall
of rock.

Tomorrow, they must find a way to raise the two dis-
abled men to the top, as well . . . and the children . . .
and the dogs. Sighing, the old woman knelt beside a
drift of sticks brought down from some distant, unseen
forest. First there must be fire and food. Always she
must make certain there would be fire and food, no
matter what trials tomorrow might bring to her suffering people.

⊰14⊱

Ayina sighed and shifted the weight of the child on her lap. It was time for sleep. The old tales would wait; for now her small clan had its own escape to make.

"Did she go up?" asked the boy. "Did all the people climb?" His Geh-i-nah was becoming clearer every day.

"When there is time I will tell more of the old story. But tomorrow we, too, have a hard journey before us. We must find a way to angle back around the ridges to the south of us, and make our way west to the place where the bridegrooms will come. The year grows older, and soon they will stand beside the crooked peak and wonder where their wives are." Ayina used the tone that brooked no argument, and all of her companions understood it.

Ish-o-tobi rolled against Sekto, and the old man wrapped him in a corner of his deer-hide blanket. Ayina stretched her aching legs and pulled her own coverings close, feeling on all sides the warmth of her people. It had been a weary day, but the gods had been kind. They had not known the terrible journeys and the fatal encounters that her predecessor's people had faced. Not yet.

The puma, rested somewhat, heard the hunters enter the canyon and raised his head. The way through the tumbled rocks beyond his lair was long and difficult. He had climbed the cliff, however, once before, when he was young and filled with curiosity.

What he found at the top was instant peril, and as he fell back among his pursuers, he made use of teeth and claws with equal effectiveness. The men scattered with yells and screams, allowing him to rush into the rubble and find the tortuous route that led out into the forested places beyond the water-worn cut between the heights.

They might follow still. He was sure now that they would, for it seemed that he had never been free of those hunters, his entire life being spent in flight before them.

When he won free of the canyon, he followed the curve of the mountain, which led, he knew, to an easier route. There, to his dismay, he found still again the spoor of the other men and the small meat that had loosed him from the cage so many nights ago.

When the sky was faintly paler than the black peaks thrust high against it, Ayina woke and rose. She made no fire, for they must be gone quickly, lest those who hunted the boy and the puma might still be behind them. It did not seem strange to her that they should run from men who might not be pursuing them, for already they had been shown a sign that this was not only possible but probable. That puma had come directly to their hiding place, and that was omen enough for a wise woman.

Even those not so wise could see the plain sign and take it to heart, for not even the child protested when she roused them and set them to rolling their blankets in preparation for flight.

She left Pulap to bring up the rear of the column on this day, keeping close behind Teala at the head of it. Something pushed her onward, circling back when a break caused by a creek or ravine allowed them to leave the constriction of whatever canyon they might be following. She was disturbed, uneasy.

She felt that this was because it would have been so much more direct to go straight to meet the Ahye-tum-datsehe. Ayina had discussed this with the old men and the young women, and all agreed that it would, indeed, be easier by far to go as directly as the mountains would allow.

If they had gone as they planned, following the route that Ayina had taken when the girls were small, the journey would have been long and difficult. Now, turned from that route by their need to flee, they must cross ranges that would test their strength and waterless stretches that would leave them weak and dehydrated. Yet they must move as close as possible into a position from which to set out to meet the Ahye-tum-datsehe, for the stars were almost into their late-summer positions.

They moved as quickly as possible all day, though they did not cover as much distance as Ayina had hoped. They had to climb out of several ravines that curved in the wrong direction, cross heights that were already growing chilly as summer waned, and scramble down steeps of rocky layers and sharp scree.

When they camped at last it was on top of a mesa

whose ragged skirts of rubble spread away toward the southeast, and that encouraged her. The dry riverbed she could see beyond the stones would be an easier trail to use as they headed toward their chosen route. Her first journey toward these mountains had come very near to this place, and she knew she could find her way.

When the child asked once again for more of the story, after they were settled for the night under the deer hides, she felt more like telling the tale than she had before. Ayina knew the value of experience, and often that of the old ones was of great benefit to those who were still young.

The climb, Pili found, was not nearly as difficult as she had thought. The secret lay in trusting hands and feet to find secure holds and in never looking down. The youngest and strongest of the Geh-i-nah went up first, dropping cords down the worst stretches of the height for their fellows to steady themselves as they came.

It took all the day and much of the night, but neither Pili nor Umforta had any intention of dividing their people in darkness. At last those who had toiled blindly up the cliff joined the rest on top and were welcomed with cooked food. The rest of the night passed swiftly, for Pili fell into the sleep of utter exhaustion, and morning came entirely too soon.

Once they were past that terrible barrier, they found themselves on a high green plain edged in the distance by mountains. The grass was tall and teemed with rabbits, mule deer, and other game. Elk grazed in the distance, and Pemayo slipped into the grass with three more hunters to try for fresh meat. That would put strength and heart into the people, Pili knew, better than anything else.

They ate well that night in a sheltered camp along a shallow stream. Here in the higher country it seemed that there had been no lack of rain, for the soil was moist and the leaves still green, despite the waning of the year. The next day Pili rallied her people, and they rose with more vigor than they had possessed since leaving their home beside that other river toward the rising sun.

Long stretches of meadowland rolled away, interrupted by clumps and hedges of cottonwood, willow, and small oak trees. Junipers dug strong toes into the rocks of the occasional stony buttes, and the air was crisp and clean, tanged with resin. The grass was drying, but they startled small herds of deer from time to time, and Pili felt that their scouts had, indeed, brought them to a place where even those who were ill would manage to survive.

At last they came within sight of a line of trees edging a canyon. This cut across the plain in front of them toward a cleft between two long ridges leading up into abrupt heights. Thick forest clothed the high ground, and rich meadows lay in the curve of the river.

One of the young women paused and pointed toward the sheltered grasslands lying in the arm of the distant range. "The wind of winter will be caught by the ridges. There should be herbs and grass seeds and water plants in the meadows and along the river. That will be a wonderful place for our new village."

Pemayo shook his head, his long dark locks flipping with the motion. "No, Omani. There are already people there, and they are fierce and strong. We will go that way. . . ." He pointed toward the south side of the reach of mountain, where thick brush and trees grew.

"We must turn here, going out of sight of any watcher from the villages set in that valley. We will climb the slopes leading up into that range until we reach the place Hanonit and Kesotat found. They will wait nearby, watching to make certain that hunters and scouts from the people below do not come there. No, Omani, we are not yet done with our journey."

Pili sighed, knowing that he had said what she was about to say to the waiting people. Without comment, she turned as he had pointed and headed down a shallow wash toward the thick cover that would hide them from any who watched. They did not need another battle before reaching the shelter of the high forest.

The Geh-i-nah came to the heights after three days of moving through pine and oak and aspen forest, up and down steep slopes, always avoiding going close to the rushing river that guided Pemayo back to his goal. Pili kept her shrewd eye on the terrain, the plants underfoot, the kinds of trees, the quality of the soil. If they moved much higher they could not grow corn, so she needed to know what wild plants were available.

When the young man led his weary people at last into a high meadow, down the middle of which ran a clear stream, the healer saw in the distance a curl of smoke. As the line of walkers and laden dogs moved out into the clear grassland, two puffs rose, and she knew that the other two scouts waited there for their families. It was safe to approach.

Her tired heart gave a thud of gratitude. Even though it would be very cold in winter, this was good country. They could survive here for the winter, which was now upon them. Already the aspens were dropping their gold about their roots and into the swift brooks that rushed down the slopes as early snows in the heights above melted in the sun.

"And that place was very near that tiny village we left behind us," Ayina said to the child in her lap.

"The people in that valley were the people who caught me," Tobi said, his eyes wide and dark in the dimness.

Even as he spoke, from someplace above and behind them came a gruff cry that echoed along the ravine in which they had camped. Ayina tensed, her arms tightening about his small body. The boy shivered against her, nudging his head into her shoulder.

"Is it the same puma?" Teala whispered. "How could it follow us? *Why* would it follow us?"

"It may not be the same. There are many puma in these mountains," Sekto wheezed. "There is no reason to believe that this is the injured cat that we sent down upon the heads of its hunters, far back on the top of that other height."

The coughing cry sounded again, closer now. Ayina rose. "My heart tells me that this is the cat that the gods have set upon our trail. Some strange fate is working here, and we are caught up in it. Those hunters, who must still be back there on the trail of the puma, are a part of it. If we are not to die in the workings of a mystery we do not understand, we must run again."

The boy whimpered against her, his head buried on her hip. The old men groaned to their feet, Pulap, Teala, and Netah tugging on their withered hands to help them rise.

Quickly, they rolled their hide blankets about the water and fire gourds, the food, and their weapons. Then, feeling their way in the darkness of the ravine, they stumbled forward, following the limping shape of Ayina as they fled still again from the unseen hunters behind them.

ꙮ15ꙮ

Ayina gasped with pain. Her arthritic knee throbbed where she had bumped it on a sharp corner of rock, and she paused and drew up her foot, trying to control the agony beneath her kneecap. Walking through a ravine whose stony layers had been weathering for many seasons was not a comfortable thing to do, but now it was necessary.

Something inside her urged her forward before the pain had eased, and she clutched Ish-o-tobi's hand and pushed ahead. The way was a jumble of grays and blacks, and only occasionally did a thin thread of moonbeam penetrate into the depths that had been worn by uncountable seasons of runoff from snows and torrential rains on the slopes above.

When they had traveled for some time, grunting and sighing when they stepped on sharp rocks or struck themselves against protuberances, Ayina stopped again. "We must have light. The bends in the canyon will hide it from any who follow; if we injure someone badly by traveling in the dark it will stop us entirely. Netah, bring me the fire pot."

The girl fumbled her way through the group to reach Ayina's side and held out the gourd lined with thick clay inside which she had fed, with bark or twigs, a clump of coals from their last fire.

"Tobi, see if you can find a bush or fallen tree with dried branches that we might use to make a torch," the old woman told the child.

He said nothing, but his small hand slid free of hers and he scampered away up the cleft, the clatter of pebbles under his feet sounding dangerously loud. As Ayina waited for him to return, she found that the old maternal instincts she had thought dead with her own children and grandchildren were returning. What was happening to the boy? Was he safe?

She suppressed her concern and busied herself with finding bits of grass and weed with which to make a tiny blaze. Netah turned the gourd to allow sparks to spill out into the nest of tinder, and before the child returned the material was almost burned away.

Tobi carried an armload of crackly branches, dead for many seasons and right for burning. Ayina bundled them together, making four torches of the batch, and bound the lower part of each with strips cut from one of the deer hides.

The others, all the while, dropped fragments of material onto the flame, and when the torches were ready there was enough fire left to kindle the first. After the deep darkness of their earlier journey, the single light seemed almost too bright. Red flickers caught sparks of mica that glittered from the ragged walls of the canyon. Eyes that seemed as bright gleamed from crannies and crevices, and occasional grumbles and chirps followed the course of the fleeing Geh-i-nah.

But Ayina was not afraid of birds or small beasts. She felt that the enigmatic gods that she had doubted were following at her heels, guiding the puma and its hunters after this pitiful remnant of her people. Her instinct was to run as fast and as far as possible, leading the old men, the granddaughters, and the child to some unknown refuge, where they could escape from this nightmarish journey.

She felt her control slipping, her panic rising. Yet she was the daughter of a strong people, old in discipline and determination. She did not allow herself to follow her instinct; instead she kept her steps even, just paced to the slowest of her companions' ability to keep up. She forced her heart into quiet, controlling its tendency to race.

The torch sped their feet, and only the old men's stiff joints held them back. Obstacles were no longer so painful, for Ayina could go around them and hold the torch to guide the rest, instead of bumping her knees painfully. They moved along the ravine, now sloping downward, which meant that they had moved across the dividing line onto the right side of this range.

The walls of the cleft grew lower and lower, until she could see over them into the tree-laced sky. Stars shone with the brilliance that told her dawn would soon come, as she led her people out of the long canyon and onto a gritty apron of weed and grass.

There Eketan and Abani fell together, sitting suddenly as if their old legs had failed them at last.

Ayina understood their helplessness. Her own body had been pushed past its limits. They must all rest, if a hidden spot could be found.

"Teala," she murmured, leaning against the grand-daughter. "Find a place for us. I can move no more."

The girl helped her to sit and then held out a hand to the child, who still hopped along with some remnant of energy. Together they went away, taking the torch with them. Ayina watched as the red spark of light dwindled to a point, then passed beyond some obstacle and was gone.

Despite the danger, despite the wild warnings of her heart, the old woman slept there on the ground among the even more exhausted old men. She did not wonder what Netah and Pulap might do or what Teala might find. If she had died in that sleep, it would have been a welcome relief.

She woke to a touch on her mouth. "Come," said Teala, whose face was visible now in the light of dawn. "I have found a hiding place. Let me help you up."

Ayina needed her strong hand, for she felt as if she had been beaten with sticks. When she stood at last, she was dizzy, as if she might fall again. Too much effort, too much haste, and too much worry had taken their toll on her.

But she hobbled after the young women as they supported the old men toward a thicket of service-berry and small oaks that grew at some distance from the mouth of the ravine. Teala had broken off branches of young leaves and piled them ready for the use of her elders. Ayina dropped gratefully onto one and again closed her eyes.

*   *   *

When she roused again, the sky was filled with sunlight beyond the interlaced branches of the saplings and sprouts forming their shelter. Turning her head, the woman could see down a long slope that spilled out onto a green meadow. The scent of the air was familiar—pine and hardwood and the odor of soil she knew. They were once more in a familiar range.

She could hear occasional muffled groans and stifled coughs that told her the men had waked, as well. At last they had rested enough to allow them to run, if that became necessary. Yet it would be foolish to move in broad daylight.

Those hunters who followed the great cat could go where they wanted, and the puma surely was in some safe covert for the time being. Yet people who did not want to be detected must remain hidden until night came again. They must creep sideward through the scrub that ran down from the slopes behind to the grasslands below until they were far enough away to give them an edge of safety.

It was dangerous to move at all, of course, and everyone understood that. Pahket grumbled under his breath as he hitched his robe about his waist and made certain his loincloth was securely tied.

Ayina smiled secretly. The old man would grumble if you led him into a place of safety and plenty. If he hadn't muttered under his breath she would have been certain he was becoming ill.

Crouching, sometimes creeping on their bellies, the small band moved cautiously through the thick growth. Ayina tried desperately to be quiet in her going, trying not to shake any sapling whose trembling top might alert some watcher who was searching for the puma. The others took care as well, and without incident they gained the shelter of a bastion of rock that had, in some long past, tumbled from higher on the hill.

It was almost noon by the time they found acceptable cover, and the sun stared down through a high layer of thin cloud. Ayina shivered, knowing that it might well begin to rain. A wetting was nothing her exhausted people needed. She managed to move into the angle formed by the boulders that hid them and settled there with her people packed closely about her.

They sat for a long while, resting, some dozing. But at last the child, who as usual was wedged between the healer and old Sekto, asked, "Why do they follow the puma so hard? Do they know we are here, and do they follow me as well?"

She patted his thin shoulder. "There are times when the gods take a hand in the affairs of men and even of pumas. This, I think, is one such time.

"Those hunters have reasons that we cannot know, but such determination means that they are following, as you told us, the needs of their own gods. The puma—who knows what dark gods the big cats know? It comes after us for reasons we cannot understand.

"But this is not the first time such things have happened to the Geh-i-nah. It happened many times, long ago in the time of our ancestors." She thought of the old tale with a shiver, for it was not a reassuring one.

"Then tell us, for it is a long time before night falls," said Eketan, behind her. "It will help the time pass, and if we old ones sleep, we know the story. The young will want to remember it, and you have not told it since the girls were children."

Ayina sighed. She would have liked to pass the time in sleep. Yet her people must be kept in good heart. She would tell the old story, although it was not a comforting one, in their present circumstances.

⤳16⤸

It had been a long time since the Geh-i-nah came from the east, driven before the drouth that gripped the plains country. Two generations had passed, and Tusani, the present chief of the elders, had begun to believe that they might live for many lives of men, here on the high shoulder of this green mountain.

Though it was too high for corn to grow tall, the forests were filled with usable nuts and seeds and plants. The squash vines prospered in sheltered nooks of rich soil, and beans seemed able to grow anyplace.

There was much game; the great wapiti, the moose, the deer flourished amid the browse of the high forest, and smaller creatures, ground squirrels, rabbits, and chipmunks were abundant. Hunters usually came home laden with meat. Seldom had the people been so well nourished, since those old days of legend when they lived far to the east beside a great river and amid teeming forest.

So it was with sudden shock that he looked down the path toward the distant bottom of the river canyon and saw the desperate dash of the young hunters who had gone downstream. Deer were plentiful at the lower edges of the forest, where the stretches of meadow ran up the slopes and bushes provided their favorite browse. Often the older boys and the youngest of the men stalked their prey there. No danger other than natural ones had ever threatened them.

But now the boys were running as if for their lives, crashing through thickets of alder and pine, keeping their balance with difficulty on the steep slope as they headed straight up the mountain. Kolapit, leading the group, his long legs bounding like those of a deer over obstacles, waved his bow over his head in a gesture of warning.

When he was near enough to be heard, the young man shouted, "Men are coming. Arm yourselves— they have killed little Sumipo."

Tusani had risen. Already the men and women of fighting age were arming themselves, some slipping into the forest to observe without being seen, some standing before the doors of the lodges, ready to defend the children who sheltered there.

Kulip, the healer, was gathering together her ointments and herbs, and Posete, the shaman, stood ready to help where he could. Kolapit panted to a stop, his chest heaving, and pointed behind him, toward the straggle of younger boys who were now reaching the village by ones and twos.

"We were moving along the brook beyond the great knob of rock," he gasped. "Sumipo was going through the brush to drive deer back toward us. We heard a shout. A man's voice.

"We heard Sumipo scream, and he ran out toward

the brook. Blood was on his breast, and there was an arrow sticking out of his back. He fell . . ." The boy drew a sobbing breath. "He fell before he got near, but I ran to help him. The men came crashing out of the forest before I could lift him. I ran, for I saw the child was dead."

Tusani spoke carefully, calmly. "How many men did you see? Tall, lean men or short, square-built ones? And how were they clad?"

"They were naked, but there was paint on their bodies—streaks of white and black and ocher. Their eyes were terrible, wide and staring, and they ran as if they were driven by something even more frightening than themselves," the boy replied.

"I think they were no taller than we, but perhaps fatter, wide in the shoulders, with short legs. But I did not stay to stare at them. I ran with the others to warn the village."

Tusani nodded. "Go and rest. Get food, for we will put out the fires and go up into the forest until we know whether those strangers followed you here." He turned to Kulip. "Have your daughters pack up your ointments and your herbs, for I have a bad feeling. There will be need, I think, before this is done."

She nodded, her thin gray braid flopping against her skinny chest. "I, too, Tusani. We have had peace for too many seasons. Not since our people came here from the east have we known an enemy who came to our lodges. The gods cannot smile forever upon us. It seems that they may have begun to frown."

She was wise, that healing woman. Tusani sighed in agreement as he began helping his people prepare for hiding and, perhaps, for battle. A child was dead already. He did not intend to risk the lives of any more.

The forest was cool, even in midsummer, for the Geh-i-nah had built high on the mountainside. Avoiding those below them had become, over the generations, a sort of game, pitting the skill of those on the heights against the watchfulness of those in the valleys. The distance was helpful, for seldom were hunters forced to come so far afield after game. It was a rich country.

Now the elder, leaving his village after so many seasons, listened hard for sounds from below, hearing nothing but the whisper of many feet on the dried duff of the sloping ground. Yet he felt, and when he looked aside at Kulip he knew she shared his feeling, that those who had killed a child would follow larger prey with even more ferocity.

He followed behind Disape, the oldest of the hunters. The man would lead them well, Tusani knew, for he had hunted the mountain about their village all his life. Still, a nagging fear walked beside the old man. This was a new enemy, and those painted men might come behind until his people were exhausted and too weak to fight.

"Disape," he said, his voice almost as quiet as the breeze in the leaves overhead, "when we pause to let the small ones rest, I will talk with you and the other elders. I have a thought, and I must see if you think the same."

The hunter did not turn, but his crest of hair nodded, bobbing the turkey feather that was thrust through the braid that hung behind him. Steadily, silently, the bare back moved up the slopes, blending into the shadows beneath the firs and pines and alders, and Tusani kept pace. His old legs had not come so far in two summers, but his will kept them moving until Disape paused to peer back at the people who followed him.

The Geh-i-nah snaked back down the mountain, for there were many hands of people now counted in the village. It would be a long while before the last stragglers came up to the spot where Tusani and the other elders waited with Disape. That was a great comfort, and Tusani dropped against the thick trunk of a pine and leaned back, his legs throbbing, his joints seeming to creak audibly.

As the others gathered about him, he considered the thing he must say to them. It was a terrible suggestion, and he knew that every one of his peers would shrink from it as he had done all the way up the mountain. Yet, given the history of his people, the thing that had been done down on the river, it was the most sensible thing he could think of.

Kulip squatted beside him, groaning as her knees popped. Posete came to rest against the same pine, and the hunter leaned above them, his eyes constantly scanning the climbing people and the distant reaches of forest.

Tusani bent toward the other two. "I think that we will not return to the village at all," he said. "Those men will find it. They will know that we have lived here secretly for many lifetimes. It will make them angry, and they will vow to kill us all for tricking them so cleverly. Do you agree?"

Kulip, wise in the ways of people, nodded, her eyes bright in her withered face. "They will burn our lodges and dance upon the ash. Then they will come to find us to serve us in the same way. We must go fast and far and we can never return."

Posete drew a deep breath, and the old chief could hear the unspoken protest that lived inside the shaman. Yet Posete was not a fool. He understood that with the death of Sumipo their entire life on the mountain had come to an end. New directions must be chosen now, for better or worse; the people must be guided into a way that would preserve this remnant of the Geh-i-nah.

The voice of the hunter floated down from above. "I know a way through the heights that will lead us into a strange world, dryer than this, yet livable. When I was a youth I went upon my medicine journey and saw it with these eyes. I found a canyon so remote, so high, and so forested that many times our number could hide there, if there were people from whom to hide.

"But there are no people there. Nearby, yes, but there were no people along that river, when I was young."

Tusani cocked his head and stared up into the smoky gaze of Disape. He knew that the hunter's eyes had seen places that no other of the Geh-i-nah had known. If there was, indeed, such a hidden place, it would be the old hunter who could lead them there.

He stared around the tight triangle of graying heads. Kulip nodded. Posete frowned. His lips tightened. Then he spat out the words, "We will go, then."

The sun was down beyond the height above the struggling villagers. Night drew in, and only the reflected glow from clouds above the looming trees lit the way of the very last to arrive at the flattish space where Disape had stopped their trek. Kulip went among them, tallying heads, using her fingers and knots in a thong to keep track of the tens.

For a time there was near panic when a pair of small ones seemed to be missing, but they turned up with their grandparents. Then the impromptu camp bustled about, bedding down, chewing dried meat and nuts and anything else brought along on this flight, for they must not risk a fire.

Watchers were posted far down the mountain as well as higher up the slopes and on either side. No subtle scout would find them without being detected, Tusani resolved, and those chosen for the duty understood the importance of their watch.

They could not help leaving an obvious trail—so many people could not move through forest without trampling down turf and deadfall and scuffling fallen leaves. Any who came after must see the way even in moonlight, it was clear.

But the old man held the hope that by the time those following came as far as this, his entire village would be beyond the mountains, in that distant place Disape promised. They must go like the wind, but they were hardy people, toughened by the rough life of the heights. What was needed, they could do.

Long before the sky turned pale above the treetops, the Geh-i-nah were again on the move. Now they were in better order, the strong helping the weak, the old carrying the very young. Burdened with hides and food supplies, weapons and tools, the line of walkers now was organized to keep any from falling behind.

At the rear came two hands of strong young men, armed and alert, keeping watch on the back trail for any pursuer. Tusani had chosen Kolapit to make one of those warriors, for the lad had done well in giving the warning. He had kept his head, and the elder would watch him now for sign of the ability to lead, which seemed to be so rare.

Tusani trudged behind Disape, keeping his gaze fixed on the hunter's broad back. It would require all the stamina he had to complete this journey. Indeed, he might not finish at all but fall beside the trail, spent in the effort of saving his people. But that was what an elder was for.

The long line of people moved through the forest to the barren heights. Above them loomed loaf-shaped peaks of stone, and there was no brush to hide them if an enemy approached. It was time to force his people to speed, and Tusani dropped back along the line, speaking sharply to any who lagged and urging on those whose age or disabilities slowed them.

He understood such things, for he suffered with them, and even those in pain understood that he knew what they felt. The Geh-i-nah pushed ahead, led by Disape, until the last of all disappeared into the canyon the hunter chose. Tusani, at the end of the column with young Kolapit, saw with relief that only someone who climbed onto the heights could see the villagers now.

He followed them slowly, helped by the young man he had chosen. When they halted at night, he rested but did not sleep, for he felt his own end drawing near. Still, he was determined to see his people clear of this danger, there in that distant place where they might be safe.

They came down again into grasslands, which turned into a low mountain range covered with forest that overgrew small valleys cupped among the heights. Clear streams ran chuckling among rounded stones that shone green and blue and ocher beneath the sunlit ripples. Fragrant leaves rustled on the small oaks and mountain mahoganies crowded along the banks, and small creatures scuttered among their roots, hiding from the intruding group.

Tusani stepped into a small clearing thrust into the curve of a brook. A pale golden buttress had fallen there from the cliff beyond the water, and he sat on the lowest part and gazed about him, his heart rising amid such peaceful surroundings.

He turned to Disape, who leaned against a higher angle of the boulder. "Will they come this far?" he asked.

"I think they will not. When our trail leads away from their mountains and across the grasslands between that place and this, they will turn back. Then they will understand that we will not return to the village we left."

Tusani felt a surge of relief. "Then we might remain here and set up another village."

The hunter sighed deeply. "No, Tusani. There is not room for so many. We may rest here for a time, search for herbs, hunt small game. But in a hand of days we must go forward. The place we are going to find will provide food and game and shelter for us, if we do not delay until many die and others are too weak to travel."

The elder had feared as much. But he managed to enjoy the few days during which he could stretch out his painful legs and cushion his aching bones upon the skins his women had brought. When he rose once again to journey forward, he did it with renewed vigor, and together he and the other elders pushed his people toward their still-distant goal.

☙17☙

Ish-o-tobi wriggled and sighed, his head lying heavily on Ayina's arm. "Just the same," he murmured.

"Very much the same," the healer agreed. She stared out of their covert into the sky, which was turning dark blue in the east as the sun sank over the mountain. Its shadow stretched over their hiding place, down its own sloping knees, out of sight.

"It is time to go," she said.

Pulap stood and shook Sekto, who had been sleeping hard, his back against a bush. Teala helped Eketan to his feet, and Pahket, grumbling all the while, roused himself and Abani and got them onto their weary legs. In the meanwhile Netah had rolled up the skins on which they had rested, bundled the bits of food left from their sparse meal, and readied the supplies for travel once again.

They did not return to the slope draining the canyon they had followed before. Instead, Ayina headed at an angle toward a heavily forested hill to the north. She remembered that hill, for she had passed it before, while leading her small band of survivors to safety after the death of her clan.

Life, she thought wearily, seemed to go in great circles like ripples on a pool, repeating the same tragedies over and over again. She wondered, as Ish-o-Tobi tugged her along by the hand, what repetitions of the old patterns awaited her granddaughters in their future lives with the Ahye-tum-datsehe.

But it was growing darker all the while, and she turned her thoughts toward leading this last remnant of the Geh-i-nah toward the place where they must wait for the bridegrooms. That was the important thing now. The girls would go away to strongly defended dwellings on that distant mesa, and she would send the child with them.

Then whatever happened to her and the old men would be as the gods willed. Their uses were done and their lives were spent. She wondered if old Tusani, generations before, had felt this same sense of fatality. Probably. Leaders were to be used to their limits.

As the last light left the highest clouds hanging over the peaks, Ayina's blood chilled. Again, the gruff cry of the puma sounded, this time from above and to the south of their route. Did the hunters still pursue it?

A sudden thought froze her heart. Was it the Tsununni who hunted the puma and the child? It had been so long since their attack upon her old home that she had pushed those fierce people out of her consciousness. Now she pulled them forward again and thought hard.

The men she had seen were not unlike them. The Tsununni looked like most people, dressed in hides, armed with bows and spears and atlatl. It was by their fierce cruelty in war that they might be distinguished. Though she had never known anything about their ways or their beliefs, she could find it in her heart to think they might well sacrifice a child to the strange gods that drove them.

If they still followed the puma, which still held to the route she took no matter how she tried to outguess it, then all of her people would die. Four women, four old men, and a boy could not hope to overcome a band of warriors whose ferocity had conquered the Geh-i-nah in their strong houses.

She said nothing of this, however, leading her people around the foot of the marker hill and down into thick forest beyond, where she turned again toward the west. The bridegrooms would come soon; her granddaughters must be at the appointed place, or all her long years of training and work would be lost.

They walked most of the night, until the old men could no longer stagger. When they halted to shelter in a thicket, Ayina knew they must risk building a fire, for only meat could sustain her charges on the last leg of their terrible journey.

She spoke softly with Teala, who nodded, took her bow, and slid into the trees. The girl would return with game of some kind; fat woodchucks would do if nothing larger could be found.

Ayina ignored her own misery as she got the old men settled on hide blankets. Meanwhile the girls cleared a space, set stones to confine the small fire, and kindled twigs, using coals that still lived in the carefully tended fire gourd. By the time Teala returned, carrying three grouse and a pair of woodchucks, there were glowing coals over which to spit the meat.

Ayina knew the old men needed broth, so when the meat was done she took the small pot she carried in her bundle and filled it with water from the bunch of gourds that held their supply. Then she found clean stones, heated them in the fire, and dropped them into the water to boil the bones.

Sekto had broken a tooth, one of the few remaining to him, two suns ago, and she knew that if he was to keep any strength he must have something he could swallow without chewing. He scorched his mouth with the hot broth, but it went down, and the other oldsters took their share gratefully.

For once, her people settled to rest with full bellies, while the sun rose over the ridge to the east and revealed the lower stretches of the forest, now swathed in mist. In the old days, Ayina would have stood watch, but now she could no longer manage that. The girls urged her to rest, while they took turns at guarding the sleeping elders.

Now the cat wavered in his tracks, his sides heaving with effort, his mouth dry, his nose hot and fevered. His vision seemed to be failing, for sometimes rocks and trees seemed to blur or to move strangely, but the puma crept onward, driven by some instinct he could not understand.

It was time to die. He felt it in his bones, his fur, his very paws. He should lie on a cool stone and drift into the darkness that even now threatened to stop his eyes from seeing.

The men were behind him, very near now. He could hear occasional talk from them, as he fought his way over stones and up wooded slopes.

The small meat was still ahead, he knew, for he could smell the tracks when his trail crossed that of those before him. But he no longer remembered why he moved or why they might always stay there, moving and moving away.

He sank onto a patch of soil, still moist from a recent shower, and felt it cool the fever in his blood. Not much. But any help was good, and he lapped a leaf full of rainwater as he rested.

When had he eaten last? A fat hare in the night, he recalled, had been too slow even for his slowed spring. Yet now he did not hunger. He felt that he might never be hungry again.

When he came to a rocky ledge lying above a long, forested valley, he halted and raised his head. This was the place. It was here that he must stop and die; all his instincts told him that.

Beyond the trees he could hear a murmur. That was the small meat and those who traveled with him. The thought came suddenly clear. The puma slitted his eyes and waited for whatever might come. The mountains, the trees, the cliffs, the waters and the rocks had brought him here. Now he must wait.

When the hunters rushed at him from the angle of the ledge, he rose, filled with a spurt of anger that overcame, for a moment, his terrible weakness. He slashed with cruel accuracy, one paw tearing a chunk of flesh from the shoulder of an attacker.

Then the spears caught his body, and he gave one last cry before the kind darkness of death took away his pain and his weariness.

Late that afternoon there was a terrible confusion of sounds in the distance. Yells, coughing cries from the puma, a shriek. Then a chant rose shrill into the clean air, interrupted by yips and shouts. Ayina woke suddenly, sat, and moved Ish-o-tobi's head from her lap.

"They have caught up with him, and he defended himself, but they have killed him," said Teala. Her dark gaze was fixed on the height to the west of their present position. "Near. Too near. But perhaps—Grandmother, do you think perhaps they will turn back now? We have left no sign on the earth to tell them we went before them."

Ayina closed her eyes and thought herself into the minds of those determined hunters. Big pumas were hard to locate and harder to hunt down. If the fur of one of the cats was needed for whatever terrible ceremony they planned, they might turn away, once they had killed and skinned the beast they had followed so determinedly.

There were other children than the boy she had found. Children were plentiful, and they died of many causes every season of the year. Whatever fate had brought the puma on their tracks, it might be that it found ease in the battle now that had taken place beyond the forest.

She was certain that she and her people had erased every track, every ash from their infrequent fires, every displaced stone or broken twig as they passed. She had personally seen that no track of the child, in particular, was left to guide those strange enemies behind them.

She opened her eyes again. "I think they will go back and find another small one to send to their gods. Now we will go fast toward the meeting place, for less than a moon is left until the Ahye-tum-datsehe come to find their wives."

There was a surge of new energy running through the Geh-i-nah now, and Ayina could feel it as a physical sensation. The end of the journey was in view, and everyone, old and young, knew that they could endure until they reached it.

Even her arthritic legs and shoulders felt better, as she took up the lead, her gaze fixed upon a distant crag of golden stone that appeared and disappeared as they made their way through the forest. Her heart thudded steadily, and she found it easier to move now.

Enthusiasm remained even when the energies of the old men waned again, and the group covered more distance than they had in days. Traveling by day was a help as well, for darkness necessarily slowed the pace. Within three suns, they were beyond the first range and going along the river canyon she recalled from her earlier journey. They would come to the crooked peak in time, she felt certain.

Ayina led the people up and over ridges, across dry flatlands, heading always toward the crooked peak that was the mark of the meeting place.

She allowed her clan to slow after a time, for exhaustion was telling upon everyone. There had been no time to gather roots and seeds, and the store they brought with them in the beginning was almost gone. Meat alone was good on a temporary basis, but she pulled up cattail roots as they crossed streams. At night she roasted them in the cook fires, and their hot flesh was sweet in her mouth.

Moving steadily but much more slowly, she brought her people at last to an apron of grass along a cliff where a spring burst from sheer stone. There her people could rest for a time, before undertaking the last leg of the journey. With some time to gather their strength again, there would be time enough and more to reach the place where the signal fires had always been kindled.

The stars on the horizon were in their familiar summer patterns, the Twin Rabbits hanging low. It was very near the time when the signal fires had traditionally been lit, and it was Ayina's conviction that the young men of the Ahye-tum-datsehe now traveled across the rough country from their high mesa home.

In this comfortable spot, she thought again of the old journey of her people to the gorge along the river that now lay not very far from this place. Settled near abundant water, with small game practically begging to be caught, she continued the old story for the ears of her granddaughters.

⤕18⤔

The way through the mountains was crooked and very long. Though Tusani had rested himself, along with the other old people among his villagers, the rough walking along the course of the stream tried him badly, and his heart lurched and pained him.

Indeed, there were broken legs and arms among the children, and at last Kulip, dashing to the side of a fallen youngster, slipped and broke her collarbone. That was a serious matter, for her services were constantly needed along the line of march.

At last Kolapit said to him, "If two of the young men could carry the healer, it would keep her from growing so weary. We have bound up her shoulder so that the arm does not swing. Now we might grip hand to elbow, hand to elbow, making a sort of seat, on which she may sit while we take her where she is needed."

It was a good suggestion, and Tusani thought with satisfaction that there was, indeed, a leader for the future. "That will work well. Just be careful not to fall with her, for she is frail and more of her bones might break," he said.

The people went on then, taking more care, avoiding more breaks, though there were more bruises and lumps caused by slips on the wet stones. At last the stream wound through a gap between two shaggy heights, and the old leader could see a long stretch of land that lay, seemingly endlessly, toward the setting sun.

Below the range they had crossed, the grasslands swelled and sank, and at some distance from the foothills a deep gorge appeared, almost invisible until you came very near. This was no small mountain river, easy to cross, but a major watercourse, deep and swift now in midsummer, when melting snow still hung on the heights above.

There on a plain baked by the sun, the Geh-i-nah halted and gathered into family groups, while the elders consulted. Tusani welcomed the rest, though he disliked the time wasted while Disape and other hunters searched for a crossing that would not endanger their people.

On the third day, he led his people toward the place the scouts had found, where the climb downward was less perilous to the limbs of the very old and the very young. He went down it holding on to the protruding rocks and digging his fingers into narrow cracks. Below him went Kolapit, stopping at difficult places in order to brace the elder's shaking body.

They lost three on that descent, two children and a pregnant woman who lost her footing at a spot where the foothold was slick with damp. It was a bitter loss for the people, for their numbers had dwindled over the past generations. Tusani grieved, but he did not slow their march.

Disape led them along a track beside the water, sometimes splashed with spray from the current dashing over rocks, sometimes wading through the shallows, until they came to a track worn into the cliff to the west. Great horned beasts had traveled that route to water for seasons beyond a man's hand-count. That deep trail was a blessing to the Geh-i-nah, as they climbed again onto the plain and started off toward the heights in the distance.

Beyond the first range, mountains swelled skyward in frightening shapes or leaned at dizzy angles. But it was their colors that stunned the Geh-i-nah.

As they came along what Disape promised was the last stream until the one they sought, Tusani kept turning to eye the swooping cliffs, striped like warriors bent on attack, yellow and white and red, that loomed above the puny line of walkers.

He recalled the old tales of the lands his kind had crossed in the long count of seasons their history recorded. There had been mountains, but none so strange as these, their shapes as abrupt as if they had been dropped from the sky or pushed up by dark gods dwelling beneath the earth.

He said nothing, however, as the old hunter turned away from the nearest of those bright cliffs and led them up another river, this one flanked by scrub and grassland. In the distance, there were sudden upthrusts of forested mountains, and cottonwoods, willows, and even pines grew along the course of the stream.

More colorful cliffs, these slightly less intimidating than the ones behind them, came into view. In two days they passed through this country and turned up a canyon that was so cool with trees and bushes and plants of all kinds that Tusani felt his heart grow glad.

"Is this the river you promised us?" he asked Disape.

The old man nodded. "I came here when I was the age of young Kolapit. There were no people here then, though to the north there are great stone villages built high on the tops of flat mountains and even set into caves in the cliffs."

"They are far away, however, and when I met a pair of them in the lowlands they seemed friendly. We made sign talk, and there was no threat.

"Unless others have come here since, there should be no one in this place. It is bitterly cold in winter, I learned from those hunters, but with such an abundance of wood that should be no problem for us."

Disape was bent now. His weathered face was gray with the efforts he had made to bring his people to this place, but his eyes were bright with pride.

Sighing, Tusani went after him along the river. Behind him came his people, exclaiming softly as the women discovered plants that could be used for food or medicine. The hunters looked greedily at the thick browse that would attract deer and wapiti, while the children laughed to see ground squirrels of many kinds scamper away before their feet.

The soil was thin, but with enough wild foodstuffs and carefully gathered pockets of rich dirt, where they might plant squash and beans and corn, it would not be hard to survive here. Fish flirted in the deep eddies, and small game of many kinds had tracked the damp soil beside the stream.

Above them many birds sang, their clear trilling making the air tuneful. Soon the young people began a quiet song of their own, blending their voices and the subdued thudding of their finger drums with the music of the birds. A more welcoming place they had not seen, even in the mountain home they had left.

But Tusani was watching the cliffs that leaned above the wide gorge. Layered stone, pale sand colored and dim gold in color, promised plentiful building material. No flimsy lodges would be enough to shelter them in the winter, he was certain. Here they would build solidly in stone, and when other enemies came they would have a stronghold to protect them.

The river itself looped and eddied, and as they traveled he spotted a number of promontories thrusting out into the canyon. *Those will make fine places to build our houses*, the elder thought, filing away each location in his well-stocked mind as they passed. *From those you can see anything moving up the canyon.*

Disape located a game trail leading up into the high forest, and Tusani waited beside his old friend as the people passed, going upward into this new homeplace. Purple flowers dipped under the attentions of bees, there on the slope beside him, and farther along a hummingbird hung before a lavender bell, probing the depths with a needlelike beak.

Tusani felt a deep sense of contentment steal through him. Weary as he was, racked with pain from the strain on his old joints, he knew that he had brought his people to a good place, where they could live in peace.

He had seen no sign of other people in many days. Surely, in such a wide land of mountains and forests, rivers and grasslands, there would be room even for others who might come after them in time to come.

The pale stone lay in slabs, ready for working. Even though his people had not built in such a manner before, the way was plain. Tusani and Nosete drew diagrams in the dust, argued over methods, but even the smallest child knew how to stack flat stones into walls and cross walls and then to cover them with poles that held up roofs of bark and brush. In the end that was the way they built.

The older women and children scattered through the forested heights, searching for herbs, nuts, and useful plants of every variety. The young people attacked a jutting wall of stone and began digging free the layered slabs for others to drag onto the promontory chosen for their first house.

Tusani made sure that the footings for each wall were scraped down to bare rock. He wanted no settling or sinking to weaken the house they were to build. Even lodges had been known to suffer from such catastrophes, when they were built on soft earth.

Step by step he and Nosete, Kulip, old Tilemita, and Kolapit designed and then tested the building of the walls. The size of the rooms was kept small for warmth, and one hand and one finger was the number of rooms he decided was best for each house. A family could dwell in each room, in very cold weather, keeping each other warm.

Before long, the young builders felt sufficiently confident of their new skills to continue without constant supervision. Then the old ones sat on a stone outcrop, beneath a tree so tall that one needed to lie flat to see its top.

With growing triumph, Tusani saw the first house go up and up, leaving space for a door here or a window there. It took a long while, but in time it was ready to level at the top edges of the walls, to make a place to lay the roof poles.

Once the walls of the first house were in place, the stonecutters moved to the next outthrust and began readying the materials for the second house. The youngsters could cut poles and set them in place, and even the very old could strip bark and gather brush for roofing their dwelling. It required young muscles and sure feet to work on the cliffsides, freeing the building stones for the stonemasons, now more skilled than they had been, to shape into another house.

Tusani, growing ever more feeble, began lying on a hide blanket to watch his people at their work. His eyes, so keen all his life, grew dim, and a haze seemed to surround the sun and the moon. His heart thudded like a stone pounding into mud, and his breath came harder every day.

It seemed that he had used the last of his energies to bring his people here. Every day that passed saw him grow weaker, though his wives simmered rich broths of woodchuck and herbs and he sipped them gratefully. Still, the old man understood that his work was completed and his life was ending.

Kolapit was too young to take his place as yet, but Nosefe promised to teach the youngster everything he knew. Kulip swore to keep a watchful eye on Ganofa, who stood in line as next in age to Tusani.

He was a good old man, gentle and sweet tempered, but his judgment had never been excellent. That was why he had never considered himself one of the elders, even though his age would have allowed him to do that.

Tusani lay against a sun-warmed slab of rock near the edge of the canyon. The sun was high, lighting the lush greens of the forest on the slopes beyond the river. Ganofa squatted beside him, staring with wide-eyed interest at the house that was all but completed.

"We have never had such houses before," he murmured in a voice like that of an ancient child. "How did you think of building that way?"

Tusani looked into the innocent brown eyes so near his own and smiled. "The children showed us," he said, knowing that the old fellow would understand that, though he would never comprehend the complex planning and balancing of stones the shaman and the elder had gone through to make their design.

"Of course!" Ganofa grinned, showing all the gaps in his teeth. "I see them play with rocks. Yes, and I used to play with them, too, when I was little. You pile them up, put one here and one here . . ." His voice trailed off into a mumble as he stacked a small row of flat chips to form a tiny wall.

Tusani watched his blurred shape moving. The sky was very pale, now, the tree above him a gigantic form holding its arms as if to protect them both.

"Care for the People," he prayed, feeling his heart race and then slow. "Care for the People."

And then there was welcome freedom from pain and the restful darkness.

≽19≼

Ayina's voice died away, and around her the pitiful remnant of that powerful people stirred, as if waking from a dream. Even the old men had remained awake, their hands touching the dogs, their eyes fixed inward, remembering those stone houses. For generations their people had lived there in safety.

"And is that where you lived?" asked the child in her lap. "Did you go there and see those stone houses?"

She smiled down at Ish-o-tobi. "No, boy, I was born there. Sekto, too, and Eketan and Pahket and Abani, all of us were born there. Our people lived there for so many seasons that you cannot finger-count them."

Teala, who had heard as a child the tales of the journey to that wonderful country, raised her head and stared into the eyes of her foster grandmother. "You have never told about living there, the houses, the families. You have never told us about your own family, Grandmother, although I know you had children. Tell us about the People when they lived on that

163

forested ridge above the river."

Ayina sighed deeply. She had avoided such tales, for they still held pain for her, but she knew that this, too, was a part of the heritage she must pass on to the younger Geh-i-nah.

"I will speak of such things, in time, Granddaughter. But for now I am weary. I am too old for the sort of effort we have made, and the old men and I must rest while you young ones explore this place and make certain there is no trace of any enemy. Look, too, for sign of a puma. That cat followed us for so long, I cannot feel comfortable that he is actually dead."

That was work the young ones relished. She heard Pulap and Netah head off toward the south, while Teala and the boy ranged westward, toward the head of the small stream that chuckled down the middle of the valley. But she kept her eyes closed, feeling the steady but weary thump of her heart, the knifelike pain in her leg bones, the drum of blood in her ears.

If she must speak of those ancient days in the stone houses, she must first gain control of the fear that filled her when she thought of the end of that life. She must learn to deal with the dreams that had haunted her for many seasons before the terror came upon her people.

It was frightening. It was difficult. But she knew that she must encounter those problems in dream, in order to conquer them.

Ayina closed her eyes.

The child Ayina skipped along the steep trail, her small feet sure upon the pale soil and the patches of scattered rocks. Beyond the ridge, just visible in glimpses between the boles of the great pines, she could see the cliffs beyond the western valley. They glowed in shades of warm ocher and pale sandy red in the morning sunlight, and she reveled in the colors and the feel of this summer day.

The basket in her hand must contain fresh plants when she reached the lower country. Already she knew which could be used for medicines, which for food, and which to ease the pain of wounds by making them into poultices. To be trusted, so young, with finding such things was a mark of the respect her skills had earned her in the moons since Susuni died.

The oldest healing woman died in the winter, leaving her clan of the Geh-i-nah with only Kalamet, who was a young woman with a small child, and Ayina herself. Both were being trained when the old woman sickened, and both felt their own inexperience when they could find no herb, no chant, no healing art they knew that could ease their teacher's pain.

The healer's breast had grown hard and painful, swelling until it seemed that it would burst. Susuni bore that with her usual stoicism, but Ayina had known how terrible it was by the look in those black eyes, the grip of the hand that had grown so frighteningly thin. She had searched for stronger plants than the willow, which when made into a tea eased simple pain but could not soothe this agony.

By then her teacher was beyond such safe measures. She needed something strong enough to bring ease . . . or death. The girl and the young woman had found the prickly apple plant, after long searching, and they had pounded its strange green-barbed fruit into a paste to spread on the now darkly mottled breast.

Ayina thought with some relief that it had helped. A bit. For Susuni had slept, more deeply than she had for a long, long while. When she waked it was to delirium, and when that ended she died.

The elders were disturbed that the young healers had not been able to help their old associate. Yet they understood that a lifetime of learning cannot be handed over to an apprentice in a day or a week or a year. So they watched the young healers closely until they were certain the pair were growing in understanding and skill.

Now the child was going down into the lowlands. She carried in her blanket, which with her bow and some arrows was rolled across her back, enough dried meat and seed bread to last for some time.

Before she returned she would travel for many miles, going down into streams to check their courses for useful plants. She would cross the desert lands where unexpected treasures could be found growing amid rocks and thorns.

This was her first such journey alone.

The forest whispered above her, the wind threading its fingers through the needled branches of the great pine trees. Chipmunks scampered ahead of her to hide among the frequent patches of rock that formed irregular steps along the downward slope. The scent of the air was fresh, making her want to skip with delight, though she was now too responsible to give way to such childish things.

Birds of many kinds whistled and trilled and chirped above, nesting now and protecting their territories. She recognized such behavior, for her own people were doing much the same.

Already her sister Tanat had brought a new husband into the stone house that was the home of their family. If Ayina was not badly mistaken there would be a new infant there before the snow flew.

That was good. The losses that the old ones spoke about when they told the tales of the journey from the east had been made good. The hand and one finger of stone dwellings were filled to bursting with families, and along the ridge many pit houses had been dug into the scanty soil, their pole-and-brush roofs made thick and warm with dirt, to protect their inhabitants from the snows of winter.

Some of the younger families had moved away from the mountain above the river their grandfathers followed when they came. New houses of several kinds were in place beyond the cliffs to the west, and there was sometimes a visitor from the new colony who came to trade gossip or medicines or foodstuffs with those in the older one.

She thought with warmth of young Nosete, who had visited with his father in the autumn before Susuni died. She had not been burdened with so many responsibilities then. The two of them had sat in the shelter of the sturdy stone walls, gazing over the canyon below, and talked for a long time of many things.

She had found to her surprise that others than she wondered *why* things were as they were. Nosete, too, had questioned his parents and aunts and uncles until they good-naturedly sent him off to perform tasks they had obviously invented just for him.

She knew that feeling, for she had been set to do

things that nobody since had ever troubled with. Who
else had swept the pine straw from the path leading
along the ridge to the next house? No other child, boy
or girl, had been sent to find specimens of every sort
of plant growing along the bank of the river. In doing
so, she had found several that were very useful, but
that had been, she understood, more an accident than
by design of her elders.

She smiled, stopping to lean against a pine. She
stood now on an abrupt drop, and below were the
tops of trees as tall as the one beside which she
stood. Beyond, across a wide sweep of flat land
dotted with bushes and crossed by occasional deep
runnels left by snowmelt, were those cliffs. Beyond
those yet again were the houses of those other Geh-
i-nah, where Nosete lived.

But her task did not lie there. She must move down
the country toward the red-and-gold cliffs that her
grandfather told about, soaring curves of stone that
were almost frightening in shape and size.

The sudden grunt of a bear sent her shinnying up
the pine tree almost before she could think. In spring
the sow bears were ill tempered, and no sane person
waited to see what mood any bear might be in when
met in the woods.

Once she reached the first lateral branch strong
enough to hold her weight, Ayina swung her leg
around and took a seat there. When she was settled
and began surveying the ground for any peril, she
found herself looking down into the face of a very
large, very angry grizzly.

That puzzled the child. She was out of the way; with
sudden comprehension, she turned to gaze about her

at the treetops on a level with hers. In the next, a big
hardwood, two young bears hugged the pale gray
branches and stared back at her with more curiosity
than fear. If she had stretched her arm very long, she
could almost have touched the nearest of the pair, for
the limbs of the two trees were interwoven where
they met.

Hah! She had never been in such a dilemma before,
and she couldn't recall hearing of anyone else being.
She could think of no tale that offered a hint of how
to escape such a situation.

Ayina removed her blanket roll from her back and
looked at the bow, the arrows. They were too weak
as to bow and too small as to arrows, made for her
short arms and immature strength, to kill the sow.
And when she looked into the button black eyes of
the two cubs she felt sure that she could never shoot
such babies, anyway.

Maybe she could force them to move, to go down
the tree to their mother. Then the family would go
away, so Ayina could continue her work.

She checked the arrow points. They were sharp but
not large. Still, she hated to think of really injuring
one of those small ones. But if she used twigs, she
thought with sudden excitement, she might be able
to make the pair uncomfortable enough to want to
leave.

Pine twigs were brittle and frail. There would be no
danger, but it might be distracting. She broke off part
of a dead branch, which hung down on the other side
of the trunk, just within reach. Scaling off the small
twigs, she achieved a fairly straight length of dead
wood.

When she strung her bow, the sow below snuffled loudly, as if inquiring what she might be doing. Ayina ignored her, sighting in on the rump of the nearest cub. When she loosed the awkward missile, it went awry, and instead of hitting the rump it grazed the ear of her target.

The cub grunted and looked about, as if for some angry insect. The ear twitched, and one round paw rose to brush it, while the small one gave a pitiful grunt.

Ayina broke off another bit of branch and aimed it at the other cub, which was farther away on another hardwood limb. Side on, she had a better shot, and her "arrow" took him in the ribs and made him flinch. He began backing away toward the tree trunk.

The bear beneath the tree was now grunting and snuffling and beginning to reach up to claw the bark of the pine tree. The nearer cub looked down and gave a mewling cry that was much like that of a human child.

Ayina sent a rain of branches toward the pair, now throwing them, for using them as arrows was too time consuming. Cones bounced off furry faces and ears, and bits of brittle pine thumped into their well-padded ribs. Now the two were moving, scooting backward along the branches. The first to reach the trunk turned and grabbed it.

The second almost pushed him off when he caught onto the trunk. Then the two slid recklessly down, bumping off intervening branches and grunting when they caught their fur on rough spots.

Their mother, waiting anxiously below, gave a rumble as soon as they were down. Then the three set off

at a ground-eating pace and were out of sight before
Ayina could recover from a fit of laughter and drop
her bundle to the ground.

It was an odd beginning for her quest. A good
omen? There was no way to know that, and the child
shrugged the question aside. She had outgrown her
terrible need to know everything when Susuni died.

The long trek down the mountain did not try her
young legs. Indeed, she moved back and forth across
the slope, as well, checking under deadfall for fungi,
picking occasional flowers just for fun, and keeping
an expert ear tuned to the sounds of the mountain.

When she came out of the trees at the foot of the
ridge, she faced a long walk across very rough country, cut with runnels worn into the sandy grit by
runoff from the heights behind her. There she went
carefully, for a rattlesnake bite, a broken leg, any real
mishap would result in her death.

No member of her family would come to search for
her, knowing that she would be gone for days. And if
she did not return at all, they still would not come;
searching for a single person in the broken lands was
a waste of time and manpower. The thought did not
trouble her mind. Death, like life, was a part of her
world, and no person she knew questioned it or feared
it unduly.

⊱20⊰

The old Ayina stirred in her sleep. She almost smiled, remembering her youthful vigor, the ease as she ran, the feel of clean wind in her face. Again she moved into that past, now only accessible in dream.

The way down the ridge was very long, very hard. But at last the child came to the river again, after taking a curving route, requiring three days of walking, around the foot of a long series of ridges.

All the way she searched for usable plants. She had filled her basket several times, emptying it at well-marked spots and tying bundles of herbs to young trees. After her encounter with the grizzly, she made certain to bind those bunches high enough and far enough out on individual branches so that even young bears couldn't move out far enough to reach them.

Then, satisfied that she would be able to gather a large supply of dried materials on her return trip, she moved down the river, now growing wider and deeper, toward the even greater cliffs that the old tales said rose along its lower course.

At the first bastion of glowing stone, Ayina paused, fascinated by the colors, the size of the array of warped and angled rock beyond the stream. The heights where she lived were cloaked with trees, and she wondered if these aggressive masters of the sky could grow even so much as a weed. There was certainly no greenery to be seen along their faces or peering over their crests.

That was, in a way, a relief. Although the cliffs fascinated her, compelled her toward them, she understood too well that for one alone to try climbing those layers of white and umber and rosy stone might well result in a fatal fall.

One day, she thought as she moved along beside them, she would come here—with Nosete? She hoped that might be so—and go with him up to those arrogant cliff tops. She would like to look down at all this country from such a height, seeing what lay beyond them as well as here where she moved like an ant among the scrubby growth, over the pale grit of the soil.

Thinking of such things, she was not listening with her usual alertness. So it was with shock and terror that she found herself moving around a thicket of young pines to face three men.

They seemed as astonished as she, and for a moment the four stood staring at each other, all of them, Ayina was sure, waiting for some indication as to whether to fight or to run. A child was usually an indication that a large party was nearby, and she knew these men would not attack her, though they might, if she did not behave sensibly, abduct her for adoption into their own clan.

"Are you Geh-i-nah?" she asked, smiling. "Or are you another people?"

The shortest of the men, burly and weathered as an old root, came forward a step and looked down at her, as if assessing her. "*E'ht Ahye-tum-datsehe?*" he asked, his tone unmistakable.

The child knew from the old tales that there were other people and other tongues than her own, but this was the first she had ever met. Her heart thudded with excitement, all fear lost, as she set down her basket and smoothed a spot in the gritty dirt for drawing.

"Ayina," she said, drawing a stick figure and then pointing to herself. She caught her tongue between her teeth with concentration as she drew several other stick figures about the first. "Geh-i-nah," she said.

When she looked up, the old man had hunkered down beside her and was studying her drawing and her face alternately. In turn, he took up a twig and drew a two-legged shape holding a bow.

Pointing to himself, he said, "Ihyati."

He sketched in neatly, as if used to drawing such things, a great shape much like that of the cliff that now reared above them. On its top he drew many shapes of people and square houses much like those her people had built in the cliffs above their own river. When he pointed to those other man-shapes, he said, "Ahye-tum-datsehe."

So. Now she knew his name and the name of his people. What a wonderful adventure to find on her first lone expedition.

She did not understand his next question, and he repeated it, together with hand signs for days. Then she realized that he was saying they had traveled many hands of days from the north, and she wondered where they were going and why they should make such a journey, when the lands were full of food plants and rabbits.

When he looked at her questioningly, she pointed to the east, which was not the true direction, and raised two fingers. This might not be an enemy, but her people had suffered too much from pursuit by strangers to risk exposure to chance-met men. A false direction and time would misdirect them, if they intended evil.

The two of them squatted together over the sketches, and Ayina wondered if the two younger men were the sons of Ihyati. But when the old man rose, he said nothing to them, though he seemed to be assessing her worth as a captive.

However, she was still very small, very young, and her knowledge of healing did not show on her face. She looked as useless as she could manage, and he nodded curtly and turned his steps toward a forested height off to the south.

They were hunting, she knew, though she wondered again that they had come so far after deer, when the country along the ridges was filled with elk and moose and many kinds of smaller game. Yet she was not sad to see them file away among the sunflower stalks and the scrub growth of small oak and pine.

If she could have avoided meeting them at all, she would have. As she had been surprised into the confrontation, she filed into her memory the name Ihyati, the tribe Ahye-tum-datsehe, and continued her travels.

Yet, even small and crude as the sketch of that distant mountain had been, something about its arrogant shape remained in her mind. She felt that, even among the myriad tormented shapes of stone that haunted this land, she would know that peak, if she ever chanced to travel there.

But she hoped that she would never be forced to go so far. This journey was exciting and eventful, but she had no desire for another.

Keeping her ear tuned for other unexpected travelers, she busied herself among the plants growing along the river. She even hopped across, using fallen boulders as stepping stones, and explored the other side of the water, under a shelving slope of pale golden stone. An occasional rattle urged her to caution, and she watched closely before she placed foot or hand on the rocky slope.

An unwary ground squirrel poked its head over a ledge of rock, still at some distance, and she froze, bending, as it twitched its whiskers and surveyed the area between the cliff and the water. It was making ready to go down to drink, she thought, and her right hand crept silently toward a well-shaped flake of stone.

When the rodent popped over the ledge and scampered down the steep slope of scree, she straightened and sent the flat bit arrowing toward the animal's neck. With a thump, it connected and bowled the squirrel over. Before it could collect its wits, Ayina brained it with a rounded chunk.

Her meal that night was ground squirrel flavored with sage and roasted over a tiny fire, which she kindled in a cup of rock, sheltered from both wind and chance wanderers. The animal was young and tender, and before it was quite done its juices, dripping into the coals, made her mouth water.

Once she had eaten, she covered the coals with a thick layer of pebbles. Then she moved away from the spot where the fire had burned and found a place in the lee of a hillock, with a stand of pine to windward. Curled into the thick mat of pine needles, she slept deeply until a magpie squawked beside the river and woke her.

She traveled for a hand of days along the course of the river, and when she came at last to cliffs so brightly colored, so tall, and so beautiful that they took her breath away, she knew that she would go no farther. There, along the wide meadows that lined either bank between the striped buttes, she found new plants, which she carefully uprooted and packed in mud to be carried home again.

Then, realizing that she would be burdened past her ability to transport so much in her hands and on her back, she went among the willows along the river. There she cut poles to make a travois, like those her ancestors had used, drawn by their dogs, when they came across the eastern lands.

She had no dog to pull it along, but she knew that her sturdy strength could pull behind her much more than she could carry. Once she reached her home country, she could hide her plunder near the bottom of the mountain crowning their ridge. Then her people could follow her down to help bring the treasure of plants and seeds and leaves up to the stone house that was the home of her family.

*   *   *

Again Ayina stirred. This time she opened her eyes and stared up into the clear sky of summer, where a hawk wheeled and the first hem of cloud was peering over the rim of mountains to the west. She had, for a short while, been young again, secure in the knowledge that her people were strong and well protected.

Even so long afterward, she shivered, for the child Ayina had not yet learned to foresee dangers to come. Her dreams had been clear and innocent and filled with light, instead of predicting darkness to come.

The old woman sat and smoothed her hair with both hands. Ish-o-tobi, who had been sitting beneath a tree, evidently watching her sleep, came to sit on the ground beside her. Refreshed, saddened but strengthened by her visit to the past, she rose to build a fire for their meal, accepting the grouse and two big rabbits the boy had brought back from his explorations.

"Teala is a good hunter," he said. "She killed the rabbits, but I got the grouse with my rock." His angular face was bright with pleasure, and she smiled, remembering a time when she, too, had been joyful over such small matters.

"Then we will cook them. Where are the others?" she asked him, as she began skinning the game.

"The men are sleeping. They made a shelter of hides and went under it, for Sekto says that it will storm soon."

Ayina looked again at the sky that was visible from their camp. Sure enough, that hem of cloud was growing wider, pushing eastward over the ridges, bringing with it rain, perhaps, even in this desert country.

"And my granddaughters?" she asked. Her hands, expert and swift, skewered the game on sticks she had gathered for just such a purpose, and thrust the sharpened butts into the ground, so as to hold the meat over the bed of coals that was already beginning to glow red.

"They went to the stream to wash. It was hot, and we got dirty, Teala and I, when we fell down a cliff into a pile of sand. The others went with her. Can't you hear them laughing?"

Ayina cocked her head and listened. Were her ears, too, growing old and failing in their duty?

The distant tinkle of laughter came at last, and she nodded. "Then we will have everything ready when they come, for when those three play in the water they forget time."

She twisted the spits so as to turn the meat over the coals. "After we eat, I will tell the story of my dream, for I lived again in my childhood, and that, too, is a part of the history of the Geh-i-nah."

Ish-o-tobi's eyes went wide with pleasure. "Another story?" he breathed. "There will be more after that?"

Ayina sighed as she tended the meat and listened for some grunt of waking from the old men or the steps of the returning girls. "There will be more, but not many will be as happy as this," she said.

Then there came a deep cough from the thicket where the old men had been sleeping, and she pushed the dream from her mind as she tended her people.

≈21≈

The cook fire had been quenched and the camp moved into the shelter of an outcrop on the side of an adjacent cliff. The thing was almost a cave, and when the cloud covered the mountaintop and light snow began drifting down, Ayina agreed that it would be safe to kindle a new blaze there.

The coughing sickness was as deadly as any enemy, and fire was a good preventive measure, she had learned long since. It was still early, but outside it was dark, and the remnant of her people were packed close together, sharing the warmth of their bodies and the comfort of their spirits.

"A story," Ish-o-tobi demanded, his small face reddened by the firelight. "You said you would tell us!"

But when she began, it was not with her dream but her waking memory. That dream had brought those old recollections to the surface of her mind, and now she saw in the flickering blaze the shapes of people long dead and houses that had fallen when she was still a young woman.

"When I had fifteen summers," she began, "Nosete came to my mother and father and asked for me to become his wife. His people lived very far from our wooded canyon, in drier lands to the west, and they had no great stone houses like ours. Instead they made pit houses, like that one we built after we fled from the hunters.

"My mother did not like for me to go so far, but there was still a healer in our clan house, and she understood that Nosete's people had lost their own and no other had showed the skill they needed. Every winter many died of the coughing sickness, and every summer broken bones and other injuries healed badly or not at all because there was no one to tend them correctly. . . ."

She had been glad when Nosete came with his kin to ask for her. This was what they had spoken about as children and planned to do when they were old enough. The gifts the western Geh-i-nah brought for her parents honored the entire clan. Nosete's people had made delicately quilled vests, beaded ornaments for wrist and neck, tanned furs of silken suppleness.

Her new husband himself had dressed and shaped a cloak of lynx fur, lining it with the skins of many rabbits. A hood of the same combination of furs could be tied at her neck with thongs, giving her wonderful protection from the colder winters to the west.

Ayina had never seen, far less owned, so beautiful a garment. She danced about her family's cramped space in the stone house hugging the cloak about her, until her sister protested that she would wake the newest of the babies.

That night there was a celebration. A fire was built before the stone house, and all her clan, even those from the most distant promontories thrust out over the river, attended.

Nosete had brought with him his uncle, the husband of his sister, and six sister-sons, all of whom behaved with great dignity as they took their places with old Etuni, the elder of all the eastern Geh-i-nah.

The young women filed into their place after everyone else was seated in a circle around the fire. Space had been left for them to group together across the blaze from the cluster of young men, and many glances were exchanged over the sparks and the smoke.

Ayina was conscious of Nosete's gaze as she filed demurely after her younger sisters, but she did not glance aside until she was seated cross-legged, with her soft deerhide skirt arranged perfectly. Then she looked, and even a lifetime later she knew that even the fire itself had not been brighter than his eyes.

The gifts had been piled carelessly beside the door of the house, but the girl knew that every member of her family-clan had seen and envied the value her new family put upon their kinswoman. As Etuni rose and approached the fire, the murmur of conversation died, and all faces turned toward him.

"This, the child of our sister and brother, has set her hand in that of Nosete, son of Telet and Kavoni. All has been properly done. The gifts have been given, and they honor our sister and her people.

"It is time to drink from the cup, to share the fur, to set hand in hand. Come forward, Ayina, Nosete." He waited, tall and solemn, as she rose and stepped forward to stand between the elder and Nosete.

Her sister brought forward a horn cup, carved fancifully to look like a woodchuck. She handled it carefully, for it was filled with herb tea compounded of all the healthful plants that grew on the forested ridges.

Etuni took it from her hand and held it out to Nosete. "Drink, Nosete, Geh-i-nah, that you may have health and many children."

Her husband bent his head and sipped from the cup. Then Etuni extended it to her, and she repeated the ritual, tasting the bitter tang, knowing that this was the turning point in her life. From now forward what would come would be a mystery that she must deal with afresh each day.

Her sister's youngest daughter brought forward the beautiful lynx cloak, and Etuni handed her the cup and took the fur. He whirled it high and brought it down to wrap both of them in its wide folds.

"Share storm and shelter, pain and joy, life and death. Put your hands together as mates, my children, and may you live long and honorably." Leaving the two of them swaddled together in the cloak, Etuni stepped back and took his seat.

Warmth rose inside the girl as she felt Nosete's strong fingers tighten about her own. Now they were truly together, for always, and no one could force them apart.

The journey toward the west was, in part, that one she had made so long ago on her first lone gathering expedition. But instead of bearing southward, Tolumme, Nosete's uncle, headed toward an odd-shaped point of rock, across rough lands that were

dry and grew only sage and a few grasses and scrubby bushes.

They traveled for three days, passing the tooth of
stone on the north. Beyond it was a shallow valley
holding a ridge with a crooked peak, and beyond that
they found a tangle of canyons, a small stream, and
the village that was now her home.

In a sheltered cup, surrounded by stony ridges, the
humped shapes of pit houses clustered in an erratic circle about a slab of rock that was obviously a
place for ceremonial fires. But now, in summer, it was
too warm for fires, and even the individual houses
showed no smoke from their smoke holes.

Ayina paused behind Nosete, looking down with
interest at the place where she would live for much
of her life. A child looked up from some task beside
one of the lodges. He rose, tiny with distance, and
waved his arms. Then he ran into the house, and
people began coming out to wave, in turn, at the
returning travelers.

Even though she was hot with walking, Ayina
unrolled her bundle and took out the beautiful cloak.
Wearing it as she came to her new home was the least
she could do to thank this generous people for their
trouble.

She put the fur about her shoulders, marveling,
even in the heat, at the silken touch of it. Nosete
touched her cheek with one finger, gazing proudly
at her in her marriage finery, and then they turned to
follow his kinsmen down the difficult track into the
cupped valley.

Then her legs were young and strong, her head
steady even at dangerous heights. She took the track

with the sureness of a young goat, and when she came to the bottom she found herself facing what must be the elder of these other Geh-i-nah.

"I greet you, Uncle," she said to the ancient man who waited there. "I bring greeting from your brother Etuni and from all of my people."

"Daughter, I welcome you. Nosete, Tolumme, it is good that you have returned. We will rejoice tonight. For now, rest. There is food, if you hunger."

But what Nosete and Ayina hungered for was not food. For days they had traveled circumspectly, controlling their desire for each other so as not to disturb their companions. Now they had reached home, and the old man read them correctly.

"A marriage lodge has been made for you. It is small, but by the time snow flies you will be ready to return to the family house, I think. There, Nosete, beyond the drying racks, is your home, for the time. Take your bride there until the sun sets and the people are ready to make you welcome."

Except for the touch of their hands and Nosete's finger on her cheek, they had not touched since the night they were joined. Now Ayina felt her heart pumping strongly, her eyes burning, her feet flying as she raced with Nosete to the privacy of their own house.

Once they were there, the door-skin, despite the heat, drawn close behind them, she turned to her husband. "It is kind of your people to provide such a house. My people do not, and sometimes the crowded room is troublesome to those who are newly wed."

He laughed. "We have more room, and it is not so hard to build a pit house." His hands were busy, and then his lips, and Ayina forgot to marvel, for quite a long time, at the generosity of her new clan.

Their days passed quickly, though they were not expected to work or hunt or heal. This was their time together, before the demands of life compelled them again, and even the children did not trouble them, except to bring food to their door.

When two hands of days had gone by, it was time to rejoin the people. Their desires were satisfied, for the time, and Ayina, long skilled in the matters of childbearing, suspected that by the end of the moon she would know that she was to have a child. All her instincts told her so, and when the time came it was true.

That did not hinder her, however, as she went about her business as healer. There were new plants, new herbs, new patients to tend. She compounded a long list of remedies, using the heavy bale of herbs and roots that she had brought with her to her new home.

Wounds healed under her deft touch and the virtue of her poultices. Sick children eased with measured drafts of willow-bark tea. In time, others of these western people came from a distance to try the skills of this new healer who had come to them, and she was so busy that often Nosete was asleep by the time she crawled into their blankets and closed her eyes.

As her body grew heavier, however, her husband became concerned at her continuous efforts. "You must rest sometimes, Ayina," he told her. "You are training young Ketala. Let her attend to the simple matters. Save yourself for the difficult things."

Once they moved into the family house, that became

easier. For one thing, the snow began falling to a depth that surprised even her, used to the great drifts that cloaked the mountain ridges where she was born. This meant that those living at a distance could not bring their illnesses to her door.

Ketala became more skillfull, too, taking much of the ordinary work out of her hands. As the winter deepened, Ayina listened to her body, and something told her that all was not well.

She dug into her bale of leaves and roots and found dried blackberry leaves and thousand-leaf. Those she crumbled together into water she boiled with hot stones and steeped for a long time in a stone cup. It was a nasty dose, but once she drank it down and slept for almost two days and nights the unease in her body quieted.

Nosete had watched over her all the while she slept, for in winter there was no need to go out into the frozen whiteness and risk all for game that might not be located and certainly was not needed so soon. When she opened her eyes, his was the first face she saw.

"I have returned, Nosete," she said. "All is well now."

His smile was all she needed to warm her to her heart.

☙22❧

Remembering those days brought a warmth that old Ayina had not felt in a very long while. The boy snuggled against her reminded her of the child she had borne to Nosete in the spring. Sohala had been her first daughter, born too soon by a bit but strong enough to overcome that difficulty.

"And you had that child," said Sekto, nodding wisely. "I recall when the runner came from the western Geh-i-nah with word of attacks on our people beyond that area. He also brought word to us that you had a daughter. Your sisters rejoiced, though your mother had died in the winter and could not know."

"Yes," she said. "It was a glad time for us, even though there was unrest on the wind. We had people straggle into our village all spring with word of an enemy who brought death and fire to their lodges. We sent runners to all who lived to the east and the south.

"There were among those people, cast adrift from their own places, even two who were of the Ahye-tum-datsehe.

"When Tolumme, who had succeeded the old Elder in the winter, realized that he had among the refugees two who were not of our kind, he asked about among his people for any who might have met such travelers. When Nosete brought the word to me, I felt that it might be Ahye-tum-datsehe who now sheltered among us, and I went with my husband to see. . . ."

Although these weary men were not those whom she had met as a child, far to the southeast along the river, the sound of their language was the same. Ayina knelt in the dust and once again drew her patterns and spoke her name and that of her people. To those she added "Ahye-tum-datsehe?" and "Ihyati."

That startled the pair, and they stared at her sharply, as if some tale among their own kind spoke of such a communication in the past.

"They come from much farther north than our people have gone," the girl told Tolumme, when she had exchanged all the information possible to drawings and sign language. "The old man I met when I was a child drew a picture of a cliff—larger, I think—and prouder than even the cliffs we know, that looms against the northern sky. These men might tell us much about those who drove them south, if we could only talk with them."

"There is no time. We must care for those who have come to our lodges and send most on their way to other villages with more room for them. There have been many deaths this past winter, and more people will be welcome to our kin," Tolumme replied.

"But what if those enemies who attacked them come farther south and attack us?" Nosete asked. "Should we not talk with them, find who and what these new enemies may be? There may be danger for us, before another hand of seasons passes."

Tolumme looked at his nephew, frowning. Though he was a good leader, skilled at managing his people when they quarreled or at trading or negotiating with the other clans of the Geh-i-nah, he was not, Ayina had soon realized, nearly as wise as old Etuni, in her former village. Thinking ahead to future problems was not a thing that he was capable of doing.

"I will talk with the women and children," she said softly into her husband's ear. "And if there is an opportunity, I will also talk with these strangers, for with drawings and the exchange of words, it may be that I can learn something even from them."

Though she worked overtime with the new-come people, delivering babies, giving infusions and rubbing ointments onto skinned spots and into wounds, Ayina learned little from the Geh-i-nah before they went onward toward the next village. The women had been too concerned with saving the children, along with a bit of food and enough hide blankets, to notice those who drove them from their homes. The children who were old enough to notice had been too frightened or had been carrying younger siblings.

Nosete found that among the men no one had any notion who these newcomers might be. They did not fight as older enemies had done, with some concern for life and dignity. No, according to those he questioned, these were men with only one intention, and that was to kill all who stood in the way, as they went about taking houses, stored food, weapon points, furs, anything, indeed, that the Geh-i-nah had gathered together.

"Those we killed were short, square people, with stripes painted onto their faces," was the best description he could get from them. When he told Ayina this, she sighed and shook her head.

"I must talk with those northerners," she said. "They are warriors, and they had no old people or children to care for as they fought and fled. Such men notice things that others do not."

So she went to the strangers, when there was time, and worked fiercely to learn words for common things, working forward from there to more complex ideas. The men seemed anxious to learn and to teach, so the young woman brought her work to the thatched shelter where they lived and pounded roots and herbs in her stone vessel while digging deeply into their language and their memories.

At last there was a day when she could ask the question that had haunted her mind. "What men are those who killed your people?"

Their answer meant nothing to her, though the sound of the name made a shiver travel down her spine.

"Tsununni."

The name had the same chilly sound as the dry rustle of a rattlesnake. "Tsununni . . . ," she mused, trying the name on her tongue. "Where is their home?"

Ku-la-ti shook his head, and his kinsman shrugged. "Who knows?" Ku-la-ti said. "They came like a wind or a drouth, seeming to drop from nowhere, in the time of my grandfather. Because of them we began building our houses in caves in the sides of our cliffs, safe from any who tried to climb down.

"The Kiyate, our old enemies for many lives of men, disappeared without any trace, and in their place the Tsununni came, as if from the gods. We are not now troubled every summer, and sometimes many pass without any sign of them. Then, without warning, our watchers on high places die at their posts, their tongues cut out, their eyelids pinned back with thorns, and we know that terror is again upon us."

"And this time you were not in a place of safety?" she asked.

"We hunted the Middle Way, far from the mesa top, far from the refuge of our homes. When we knew the warriors of the Tsununni were approaching from the lowlands, their scouts already in place along the cliffs, we came south, hoping to find a hiding place until it is safe to go home again."

"And no one has ever understood why they came or from where. . . ." She had guessed as much. Her own people had traveled across wide lands, over harsh deserts and difficult mountains, driven by sickness and famine and enemies. It was probably the same with these new enemies. Those were the things that moved people from old countries to new.

"How do they fight?" she asked, knowing that this would be the first question Tolumme asked her.

"To the death," Ku-la-ti said. "They do not feint and retreat, and they do not use ambush, so far as we know. They come with weapons dipped in blood, faces painted with black and ocher, and they come always to kill or drive away those upon whom they prey.

"Our ancestors suffered much until they learned how to deal with the Tsununni. Then our people invented new tactics, built our houses beyond their reach, and became as cruel as our enemies, for that was necessary if we were to survive."

Ayina thought for a moment, her hands moving the mano, crushing the herbs without pause, her mind busy. Something terrible must drive these people—or they simply loved to kill. There was always that possibility, for she had known a few of her own kind, in her short life, who posed a danger to everyone because of their thirst for blood.

"And what of their families?" she asked. "Where are their villages? Surely they do not keep their old ones and the children constantly moving over the countryside."

Ku-la-ti, squatting on his heels, shifted his weight uneasily. "Many seasons ago, Uhtatse, wisest of all our Elders, moved as a sprit down the country and saw the Tsununni as they came toward our mesa. Their families were with them, children, babies, but there were no very old ones.

"When they came against us, in that time, we were ready because of his warning. Yet it seemed that the very gods were listening to our chants for protection, for devil winds dropped down from the cloud, even while the Tsununni reached the tops of our cliffs and attacked our warriors.

"Uhtatse, listening and feeling and smelling the air, warned us in time, and we dropped into crannies or hid under rocks, while the terrible storm raged over the mesa. When all was quiet again, the Tsununni were broken and scattered and many lay dead beneath

uprooted junipers or stones that had been moved by
the power of the winds. The wails of their women, left
behind in the forests below the mesa, came to our ears
for many days."

Ayina felt her breath catch as she leaned forward,
listening with awe to the tale. A people so fierce that
even the gods fought against them were almost beyond
her imagining.

Ku-la-ti shook his head and sighed. "After that
it was many seasons before anyone heard of the
Tsununni again. By that time we had secured our
cliffside homes with devious footholds cut into the
stones. We had invented ways of watching and fighting our enemies. Never again was our mesa in such
danger, although in time they began to attack us more
often."

Ayina glanced down at the mess in her worn
metate. The herbs were mashed, and it was time
to steep them to make tea for those suffering from
fevers. She would have liked to remain and talk more
with these strangers, but her duties demanded that
she go.

She rose to her feet, holding the metate against her
hip. "You are a wise people," she said to Ku-la-ti.
"To learn a way of dealing with such terrible foes
is the mark of that. Perhaps the Geh-i-nah will also
be wise. . . ." Then she shook her head in turn and
sighed, also.

Tolumme was a good man, but he could never
be called wise, she knew. If he could be persuaded
to post guards at a distance up the arroyos and on
the heights, it was the most she and Nosete might
expect.

As she marched away to the fire where her round stones were heating, she was thinking hard, but all her thoughts were foreboding. The new family, her baby, her man, all were now in peril, she felt in her bones.

⤫23⤫

Days passed as the remnant of the Geh-i-nah crossed the difficult country, drawing nearer to the crooked mountain where they must meet the young men who would marry Ayina's granddaughters. No enemy showed himself; no puma shattered the evening with its gruff cry. After their tense weeks of flight, this uneventful journey seemed tame, and even the old men begged for more tales from the past.

Every evening, Ayina settled before the small fire that held away the chill of the high desert. Then, with Ish-o-tobi in her lap or leaning against her shoulder and the dogs snuffling in the shadows beyond the fire, she retold the old story that was beginning to come more freely now, after so many seasons of neglect.

The spring passed into summer and again into fall. Snow covered the heights and began to whiten the flatlands as well, but the Tsununni did not come into the lands of the western Geh-i-nah. All of those who lived to the north and west had come and gone, it seemed, leaving their lodges untenanted behind them.

Among the last were a handful of strangers, whose tongue was not even that of the Ahye-tum-datsehe. It faintly resembled Ayina's own, yet it was different enough to be hard to understand, even to one who had learned another language already.

Again, she took her work to the shelter raised for their guests, listening, drawing figures in the dust, asking and telling, until she had some command of this different tongue. Then she was astonished, for the tales these people told resembled those she had learned from Etuni and her mother.

They, too, had come from the rising sun, fleeing from a succession of enemies over many generations. They, too, had found a refuge and built in stone, although when Pelykit drew a picture of his lodge in the dust she was puzzled. When she shook her head, he took a twig and drew in great detail the shape of a tall house, made of stone layers, which he sketched in carefully.

She pointed to the nearest of the village lodges, whose rounded door faced them. "Door?" she asked.

Pelykit shook his head. "No doors," he said. He drew parallel lines, joined at intervals by crossbars. "Ladders to the top. Then we pull them up to keep enemies out."

Ayina was puzzled. Tall houses with no doors should be impregnable. "How?" she asked.

Pelykit looked at her for a moment, and she could see remembered fear, remembered pain in his dark eyes. "We held them away for long, long," he said.

"There were tunnels"—he had to draw again before she recognized what he meant by that word—"so people from the surrounding lodges could come safely into the towers when danger threatened.

"It was good, and we stored much food there for those times when we all sheltered inside. But the Tsununni are not fools. They came and they came, summer and fall, summer and fall, and always they were unable to defeat us.

"But this spring they had gone away to think long, and someone among them had made a plan. They sent fire arrows high, to fall on the wooden tops of our towers. When those burned, the roof fell inside, bringing down each interior roof as well. People were burned and crushed, with their weapons clenched in their hands.

"Those who managed to stay on the tower tops, shooting at the enemies below, were burned alive as the flames rushed up from the shafts. We saw, for we were above, hiding along the cliff, unable to help our families as they died."

Ayina shuddered, thinking how terrible that must be. The thought of being trapped, watching her house burn, knowing her children were inside, sickened her, and she reached to touch Pelykit's shoulder with a comforting hand. Such a thing was too dreadful to think about, and she gathered up her herbs and her tools once again.

"I will go now. I wish you well among the strangers to the south. Tolumme has not often listened to the tales of our guests, but yours is one he will hear, if I must hold him while I tell it. Perhaps your tragedy will help my own people to survive."

As she moved away, she thought about a way to make Tolumme see that the continuing seasons without direct threat to their own village did not mean that danger would not come at last. But he shook his head when she spoke to him.

"We have lived for three summers since the people began to come to us. Your son Nitipu is walking now, and we have seen no enemy, heard no suspicious birdcall, known no peril except the ones these strangers tell about.

"Keeping watchers posted in every direction all of the time is not necessary now. We are safe, for we are too far away to be troubled by these Tsununni. We are many, well armed, and if they should chance to come here we will drive them away." His face was calm, as always, his chin set.

"Tolumme, those fierce people stop only when *they* will it. I have spoken to those strangers who came with the very last who fled. They tell of tall stone towers being burned from above with fire arrows. They tell of watching while their families burned, unable to climb out or even to take into death those who caused the burning.

"Those Tsununni failed many times before they succeeded. They went away to think, to plan, to make the things they needed to defeat the tower people. If they come this far, they will sweep us away like dust before the wind. We have no stone towers. We haven't even stone walls like those of my own clan's houses." She found her hands clenching, her voice growing tight as she pleaded.

"We have only our hands and our hearts and our weapons. Think long, Tolumme, before you leave our village unprotected by constant watchers and armed guardians set on the cliffs above us."

But she knew that her words had no effect. Her husband's uncle was like the rocks themselves. His thought did not change until it was forcibly changed, and with this enemy, that would be too late.

Again seasons passed. No more refugees came southward, and Ayina was certain that was because no people other than the Tsununni, or perhaps a few pitiful remnants of other kinds hiding out in the arroyos, still lived in or ranged over the mountains and the sagebrush country to the north. Possibly the Ahye-tum-datsehe, in their cliff houses, remained, but if so, they sent no messengers or refugees to the land of the Geh-i-nah.

Her third child, Setichi, a son whose smile cheered all who came near, was born the winter after she spoke with the tower people. And Tilepita, another daughter, came two summers after that. Four children, all bright, all good tempered, all beloved to her and to Nosete, now warmed their lodge, which was a new pit house they had built large enough for their growing family and Nosete's ancient grandmother.

Busy with her own family's needs and her work as healer, Ayina allowed her concerns to drift into the back of her mind. Life was busy and difficult, and sickness and injury plagued her village, as it always had and probably always would. A healer was, by definition, always occupied.

So it was that when the danger swept down upon her people, she, too, was taken unaware. For a moment, when the long scream sounded from the ravine below the village, she wondered who had fallen.

Then a chorus of shouts told her that this was no ordinary accident. A flash of memory raced through her mind as she turned toward her own house, where her children were attending to their tasks and watching young Tilepita.

Tsununni!

She could see, behind her eyes, the blazing tower that Pelykit had described. She could hear in her mind the screams of burning people—she dropped the bowl she had been holding and ran toward her house now, shouting for Nosete.

A man staggered backward into view, beyond the last of the erratic circle of lodges. He clutched a shaft that had gone entirely through his upper arm. Ayina's first instinct was to run to him, to help him, but she turned away toward her own house. Her children came first, even before her healer's work.

"Nosete!" she shouted again, and this time there was a distant whistle, their own signal. He was beyond the village, in one of the arroyos that ran into the canyon along which the stream flowed.

Relieved that he was still alive, she dived into the low doorway of their pit house and caught up Tilepita, who had been staring out curiously at the chaos that even now was spilling into the village. Sohala, who now counted almost eight summers, had already herded the small boys into one side of the house and was rolling hide blankets and telling them what foodstuffs to pack into them.

The grandmother was gathering up all the healing herbs she could stuff into a woven bag, and Ayina was grateful for the old woman's good sense. "Silipa, that is good. But you must go now, for the fighting is coming near. The children must go with you into the rough ground beyond the stream."

The ancient woman nodded. She had lived for more time than almost anyone else in the village, and only her own reluctance had kept her from being one of the Elders. Now she caught the hands of the boys, while Ayina looped the carry-thong of her bag about her shoulders.

Sohala had tied bundles of food and blankets to the children already, and now, burdened with a large bundle of her own, she caught up Tilepita. "Will you go, Mother?" she asked, her eyes bright with concern above the baby's dark hair.

Ayina shook her head. "Our own people will need help. Your father is out there, and I will stay until he comes. Go with the grandmother, my daughter. Go south and east, toward the great ridge I have told you about. My sisters and other kinsmen live beyond it and the desert and still another ridge. If you go so far they will help you."

Again she turned to Silipa. "It is best, Grandmother, to keep going, I think. These are not ordinary enemies, and they will not retreat, if the stories told by those others are true. Take the children to my people, if it is possible. If not, then hide among the arroyos and in the heights, wherever you can find enough water to survive.

"It may be a long time before we are able to come looking for you. It may be—" she looked deep into those knowing eyes—"it may be that we will not come at all. May you fare well, grandmother of my husband."

"I will take care of the young ones as long as I breathe," the old woman assured her. "But now we must go. Run, children! Race with your grandmother!"

She set off at a surprising pace, considering her age and the frailty of her bones. The small band dashed from lodge to lodge, avoiding struggling clusters of men, hysterical dogs, and frantic turkeys, which flapped, gobbling, in all directions as the battle overran the village.

Ayina caught up her healing bag, kept ready for emergencies, and her obsidian knife. That had been a gift from one of the refugees, from whom she had cut a deep-sunk arrowhead. The obsidian had been so much finer and sharper than her flint knife that she had used it instead. In gratitude, the man had presented it to her.

She thrust a lance through the loops of the bag at her back. Then, knife in hand, she ducked out of the door and darted toward the spot from which Nosete's whistle had come.

A stocky shape came toward her, lance already aimed for her heart, but she dropped to her knees and thrust beneath the weapon into the guts of the warrior. He raised his weapon again, though he reeled on his feet. She raked with her keen glass blade at any part of him she could reach. He went to his knees, then folded over onto his face.

She left him instantly, heading toward the branch of the arroyo that had been Nosete's destination when he left to hunt. She whistled, for the level of shouting had grown so loud that another shout would not have been heard. The shrill sound rose above the noise, and

echoed off the overhanging cliff beyond the stream
and up the tangle of ravines leading down into the
canyon.

This time there was no reply. Her heart cold within
her, Ayina moved forward, searching for her husband
among the dead who lay in her path. Almost absently, she cast her spear at the emerging shoulders of a
stranger as he came into view, climbing up from the
bottom of the canyon. He yelled and fell backward,
taking her weapon with him.

She caught up another, lying where a dead man
had dropped it, and went forward again, taking the
high path that led along the middle of the stony wall
bordering the arroyo that was her destination. It was
clear that the enemy had crept cautiously toward the
village along the bottom of the canyon, hidden from
any watcher above.

A familiar shape lay across the path, and she bent
over it, turning the face so she might see . . . Tolumme,
his lack of foresight no longer important. It was too
late, both for him and his people.

She let him flop back, boneless in death, and sprang
over his body. Nosete had gone with his uncle, that
morning. If Tolumme was here, then her husband
must be somewhere farther along, for she had seen
no trace of him as she came from the village.

If he had fallen into the bottom of the arroyo it
would make a long search. Ayina grasped her knife
more firmly, concentrated upon watching and listening for any threat, and began to cover the tumbled
area, bit by bit. If Nosete was here, she would find
him, or she would die in the attempt.

ϟ24ϟ

Ayina could feel the child shivering against her, so caught up in her story that he felt the terrible foreboding she had known all those seasons in the past. "Did you find him?" he asked. "Was he there?"

She could see the same question in the eyes of those about her. Even the dogs had gone quiet, their chins on their paws, their tails still against the ground.

"It grows late," she said.

But Eketan shook his head. "There is nothing to do until the sun has moved into the correct quarter of the sky when we must go to meet the Ahye-tum-datsehe. Tell the tale, Ayina. We never knew what happened to you, there in the west where your other family lived."

She gazed off toward the mountain that thrust a rounded shoulder, now black against dark blue, into a nest of stars. Living that old time had made her feel strangely young again, forgetting aching bones, teeth that twinged when she chewed, and fingers that seemed to be losing much of their old deftness.

She nodded and pushed another dead branch into the fire. As the little blaze flickered again to life, she continued her tale.

Echoes of yells and blows and terrified screams of children followed her as she sped along the ledge path that followed the arroyo, some man-heights up its eastern wall. This was the end of her village and the life of this marriage clan into which she had come. Even as she avoided stones and brush, treacherous lengths of trail, and loose patches of earth, she understood that whatever she might find at the end of this track, nothing would ever be the same again.

She paused, hearing footsteps running lightly behind her, beyond the last angle she had negotiated. Turning toward the cliff, she dug her fingers into cracks and her toes into crevices and began to climb swiftly as a lizard. When she was level with the boulder whose thrust had formed that angle, she edged back to its level, turned cautiously, and waited, braced now against both cliff and rock.

Knife in hand, she dropped onto the brown shoulders that came into view, smashing her pursuer to the narrow ledge along which the path ran. With a wriggle, she was on his back, pulling his head toward her, drawing that keen glass blade across his throat. Blood gushed over the pale dust and her own skin-shod feet, but she rose without thinking and went on.

When she came to the first dead Tsununni, she knew she was drawing near to Nosete. This one was skewered with an arrow fletched with feathers of the saw-whet owl, Nosete's favorite fletching material. She stepped over the lax body, to find the way beyond

it marked with blood and clawed places where someone had gone over the edge into the depths of the
arroyo.

She knelt and peered downward. The sun had
crossed the sky and the shadow of the western cliff
lay over the littered bottom of the cleft. In the light
reflected from the wall on which she knelt, she could
see a darker patch where a body lay strained backward
over a boulder, face to the sky.

It was not Nosete. Drawing a deep breath, she rose,
cleaned her knife with a tuft of grass that grew in a
nook of rock, and edged onward, for here the path had
narrowed to just enough passage for a single person
moving sideways.

She knew this way well, and she managed to move
quickly, although she never relaxed her attention to
any possible sounds on her back trail. Feeling with her
foot, she checked the security of the next stretch of trail,
which hooked sharply around a prow of stone. Though
pebbles and clods rattled down, the path itself seemed
steady, and she moved around the obstruction.

Nosete lay propped in a stony niche that ran down
the upper cliff to crease the path at his feet. His eyes
were closed, and his color was like clay.

She darted to his side and knelt again, laying aside
her knife and pulling her bundle from her neck. Touching his throat with cautious fingers, she found a faint
pulse there, warmth enough to show that he lived.

"Nosete," she whispered into his dusty ear. "Nosete,
I am here."

He stirred and a faint groan came from his lips, but
his eyes did not open. Ayina checked him for wounds,
for she could see no arrow or spear sticking into his

flesh. Long cuts showed that he had faced a man with a knife, though his own flint blade was missing from its sling.

Her heart faint with dread, she felt softly around his body. In his other side, slightly to the back and above the waist, she found a deep stab wound, from which air whispered against her fingers as he breathed.

Ayina went cold, for she had dealt with such wounds in the past. Sitting back on her heels, she stared at his blue-gray face; the betraying trickle of blood from a nostril and the corner of his mouth told her that whatever Tsununni had died in giving him that wound had also caused her husband's death.

Even with the edge of warmth now sliding up his body as the sun moved down the sky, he was chilled, and she carefully wrapped herself about him, trying not to cause pain. He grunted; at last he opened his eyes and saw her.

"Ayina," he said, his voice a rasp in his throat. "You came. I am . . . glad."

She bit her lips to keep from wailing. This was no time for tears. With the enemy between her and the children, her husband dying under her hands, she knew that she must keep her mind clear and her senses sharp.

But she bent over him again, touching her lips to his forehead. "My husband," she murmured, "it is a good day to die. You have fought well, and our children have gone to hide with your grandmother. When I find them again, we will all go to the house of my clan, where we will be safe from the Tsununni—for a time."

He struggled to sit up, but she held him still against her shoulder, now, feeling his body tremble. A thin note came from his lips, and she knew that he was singing his death song, greeting those of his people who had gone before him. She watched his face, but he seemed to stare past her, his eyes widening and a hint of surprise lighting his expression.

The feeble notes wandered through the arroyo, echoing dimly from cliffs up and down it. If any Tsununni hunted for them, he would hear it, but she did not concern herself about that. In this narrow place, she could fend off an enemy with rocks alone, at need. Now she must see her man into death and place his body beyond reach of the predators that would come to snarl over the dead.

Nosete's brown hand moved to touch her arm. She caught his fingers and held them, as he breathed once, twice, trembled sharply, and went still. The tang of urine in dust told her that Nosete, father of her children, friend of her youth, had gone to the Other Place.

She glanced forward along the path. Beyond the next buttress of stone she remembered that there was a crack leading down into darkness. It was narrow, straight, and no animal that she knew could climb in or out. Ayina nodded and stood, catching Nosete under the armpits.

Stepping backward with much care, she dragged him along, around the crook in the way, and laid him flat beside the crack. More rock had split away from the cliff since she had last stood there, and it was wide enough to take him. She pulled him past, guided his feet into the crevice, and gently slid him forward until, with a rush of air and a grinding of pebbles, he was gone.

She struggled with a slab of stone that half lay and half leaned onto the path. Once she had loosened it, she manhandled it, sweating, to the crack and pushed it over the opening. Nosete was sealed into his grave, and only lizards and scorpions would ever visit him there.

Ayina did not retrace her steps along the cliff path. Instead, she secured her bundle, her knife, her borrowed spear, as well as Nosete's bow and two remaining arrows, and began to climb the height to the mesa top. It was dangerous work, but she knew that there would be triumphant Tsununni exploring every hiding place near the village, searching for any remaining Geh-i-nah. Death by falling into the canyon was far preferable to any these enemies might offer her.

The sun was strong on her back as she rose out of the shadow. The stone itself was hot, but her calloused hands and feet were tough, and she ignored the burning and the abrasions as she clung and slipped and sweated. At last she reached upward and felt the edge of the cliff, with dried tufts of grass curling around the rim of rock that leaned outward at that point.

Her fingers hooked around a juniper trunk, and with her other hand she reached high and found purchase among the stone knobs at the top. Then, slowly and cautiously, she raised herself until just her eyes peered over into the land beyond the canyon.

Off to the south there was smoke—not the usual neat columns that rose from the village, to be swept sideways by the prevailing wind, but great billows that darkened the whole sky and filled the distance with blue haze. She could hear nothing but the song of wind through the teeth of rock, but she knew that the enemy must be yelling their cries of triumph in the home of her husband's people.

She could not return there. If the grandmother had been able to take the children away, she would be heading for the shelter of the stone houses to the southeast. She knew the old woman too well to think that she would remain near the scene of the defeat of their kinsmen. That being true, Ayina understood that she must make a wide arc and head for her old home, hoping to cut the tracks of her children.

She pulled herself up and went flat on the surface of the mesa. It would be foolish to risk being seen after escaping, so far, from her enemies. Beyond the game track that followed the rim of the cliff the scrub grew taller, and she slithered across like a snake and went into the scanty cover.

A bird shot out of the top of the growth and Ayina froze, hoping that no scout had noted it. But there was only the hiss of breeze through the prickles and leaves. After a long moment, Ayina crept forward, taking care not to move the rabbit brush to betray her position. With the shadows stretching longer and longer ahead of her, she crawled toward the east and the darkening sky beyond the distant ridges.

By the time it was fully dark her hands and her knees were raw, the skin abraded by thorny growth, grit, and the inevitable sharp rocks that littered the top of the butte. At last she lay flat under a scrubby pine, hidden as well as possible from any enemy who might pass, and closed her eyes.

She must rest, if she was to have the strength to find her family and cross the harsh country between this place and the ridge above the river where her people lived. From her bundle she took strips of soft deer hide and wrapped the battered hands and knees, both to slow the loss of blood and to keep from leaving a blood trail when she moved forward. In the darkness she could not see her own track, and by day some roving Tsununni might well use it to guide himself to fresh quarry.

She closed her eyes firmly, determined to sleep, but she could see only Nosete's face, clay blue in death. When she turned onto her side, her head on her arm, the picture behind her eyes shifted. Now she saw the struggles that had taken place about her as she sped toward the arroyo. At the time she had paid them no heed, but no motion was lost to that inner eye that noted everything and seemed to forget nothing.

She opened her eyes again. Sleep was impossible, but she must rest if she was to find her people. So Ayina stared through the skimpy needles of the pine into the vast deep of the desert sky.

The stars burned like small fires in the midnight bowl of blue, for the moon had not yet risen. She thought of Susuni, her old teacher, pointing out the people of the sky—the hunter, the twin rabbits, the little sister, the corn woman, trailing a cornstalk behind her. One by one, she picked out the patterns she remembered, and as she named them her eyes closed at last, and she slept.

Teala had moved close to Ayina's shoulder, and her eyes gleamed in the light of their small fire. "You were all alone there? You did not know where the children were, or the grandmother . . . I would have been frightened."

The old healer smiled. "We are all alone here, the very last of our people. We do not know when the young men *will* come, exactly, or even if they *will* come to this place beneath the crooked peak. There are more of us together, but our situation is little better than mine was."

Sekto grunted. "Now we are old, most of us, and it no longer matters whether we live or die. Soon enough we will find the Other Place and leave the world and its worries to you young ones. That is a comforting thought, though it will be many seasons before you understand it."

Ayina nodded. "That is true, children of the Gehi-nah. Now it is time to sleep. At least we are not surrounded by Tsununni, though I wonder still if those who came up from the lowlands were warriors of that fierce breed."

Ish-o-tobi's head was heavy on her arm, and she laid him carefully on the blanket before the fire and stretched herself beside him, while the rest made themselves comfortable in the sheltered niche that held off the chilly wind of the desert. But even when she lay with her eyes closed, Ayina still saw the face of her long-dead Nosete and heard the clamor of the battle that had destroyed her village, all those many seasons in the past.

≫25≪

Although the remnant of the Geh-i-nah kept close watch, there was no sign of the puma or the men who had followed it. It almost seemed eerie to Ayina, that lack of a reason to look behind and to listen to every sound carried on the wind.

Indeed, the time spent in that mountain meadow seemed too peaceful to be a part of the world she knew. As the sun moved in its course toward its late-summer position, she urged her people into motion again, but she hated to leave this place and this time of ease. She could see that the others also would have liked to stay, but they all understood that this could not last and winter would bury them here without stores of food or the possibility of survival.

So they moved away at last, taking the route that led between two of the mountains that ended their meadow. Even so high, it had become dry as the hot season passed, and already the aspens along the way were turning yellow. As they climbed, spruces raised their pale blue cones against the warmer shades, and

214

Ayina found within her heart a faint echo of her childish joy in color and shape. The boy, too, seemed to
revel in this new journey, picking up bright pebbles
along the creek they followed or stopping to admire
purple spires or yellow clusters of flowers growing
among the rocks and trees.

She watched him, flitting back and forth like a skinny bee as they moved toward their goal. When he
tired at last, he came back to cling to her hand.

"Tell the story," he begged. "Tell it so the others
can hear."

But it required all her breath to climb the steep ways
they must follow, and only when they were camped
once more for the night did she go forward with the
old story.

Only when Ayina had crossed the rough ridges to
the east of the old village did she feel it safe to travel
upright and by day. Then, despite her battered condition, she ran as often as she could find the energy,
keeping always to such cover as there might be. Here
there was scrub pine and juniper at intervals, so she
could drop, panting with effort, into cover to rest for
the next mad dash toward the southeast.

From time to time she caught a glimpse of a signal smoke off to the west, and she wondered if the
Tsununni who had destroyed her village were call-
ing in more of their kind to share the supplies that
had come with their victory. There were, she knew all
too well, good stores of wood and dried meat, carefully gathered seeds and roots and herbs that should
have carried the Geh-i-nah through the coming winter.

She did not waste her energies upon such worries, however. She moved cautiously when she had to and ran when it seemed safe. And at last she found a small footprint in the lee of a boulder.

It might have been that of another child, fleeing from the loss of home and parents, but she knew the crooked big toe. It belonged to Setichi, her second son, for she had set the broken toe herself and watched the healing to see if the injury might have long-term consequences.

If Setichi was here, then the others must be with him. She noted the direction of the track. Only the intervening rock had kept the wind from scouring that print away, and taking that as a sign, she watched the downwind edges of others as she made her way through a tumble of stones.

On the other side of that rough stretch there was a long valley of good grass, beyond which rose a crooked peak . . . the same one she had watched as she came with her new husband to the home of his people. Now she knew fairly accurately where she was with regard to her old home, and to her relief the grandmother seemed to be keeping to the right direction, if Setichi's footprint was any indication.

From time to time she found another sign, a tuft of grass that had been stepped on or a bit of rabbit-brush that had been pushed aside and hadn't straightened properly. They were ahead of her, Ayina knew now, and she wanted to rush.

Yet she had seen the end of the village, the end of Nosete, and she knew she mustn't hurry. Hurry might mean her death, or even theirs. Eyes and ears alert, she moved even more cautiously than before, which was the reason she found the dead child hidden beneath a patch of disturbed juniper.

Her eyes felt dry and strained and her heart burned as she bent and pushed aside the prickly foliage. Its strong scent filled her nostrils as she stared into the face of Nitipu, her first born son.

The death wail rose in her throat, but she quelled it, for when she touched his face it was still faintly warm. The arrow that had claimed him had been broken off, but the stub stuck out of his small chest still. His killer walked at no great distance, it was clear.

"My son," she said softly, "greet your father in the Other Place." Then she released the juniper, hiding him again, and turned toward the southeast.

Tsununni had trailed her people, that was plain. Now—she studied the gritty soil beyond the junipers—now the fugitives ran without taking care to hide their tracks. Indeed, even as she started to run herself she heard a distant twitter that was a signal from one hunter to another.

She checked the bowstring as she ran, knowing that she had only the two arrows that had remained to her husband. The obsidian knife, however, was tireless in its thirst for blood, now that she had seen her murdered child. She knew that she must approach the rear stalkers silently, and she must take them out one by one before those ahead knew she was there.

The valley narrowed between wooded ridges, and Ayina moved to the east, taking advantage of every scrap of cover. Once she was on the side of the chosen ridge, she paused, hidden among rocky outcrops, to observe the country below.

Farther along the same slope she saw a gray bird shoot upward. Ah. One of the trackers must be there, which might mean that the grandmother had led her charges into the wooded heights.

That was a good move, for the old woman must be exhausted, and the children's legs were too short to keep ahead of grown men. Perhaps she could find a place to hide . . . but no. The person Ayina knew would keep going until her heart burst with her efforts.

Now cold with purpose, the woman moved ahead, her crouching steps silent, all her senses intent upon the man she glimpsed as she slipped from tree to tree. When he paused, his head cocked to catch another twittered signal, she came upon him from behind.

At the last moment he heard something. It might have been the changed voice of the wind as it moved past her body, or it might well have been pure instinct that brought him about to face her.

He was square, as were most of the Tsununni, his bare shoulders brawny, his face painted with vertical stripes of black and ocher. The eyes narrowed, and he brought up his knife hand as she approached.

Instead of feinting or backing away, Ayina, filled with madness and fear for her children, sprang upon him like a puma and her hurtling weight bore him to the ground. His knife stabbed at her arm, but she ignored the pain.

Staring down into the dark eyes beneath her, she brought a knee up into his crotch. He spasmed involuntarily, and her knife found the notch in his collarbone and plunged to its thong-wrapped haft. The body plunged under her, twitched, and went limp.

They had, strangely, made little sound, and the wind moving in the treetops and whistling around the stony ridges had hidden even that. Now Ayina went faster, watching for another of her enemies.

As she crossed a barren knee of rock running down the side of the ridge, she dropped flat and crawled. Once she was beyond the most exposed part, she took the time to check the terrain again, and there was another dark shape moving through the scrub farther down the slope. Changing her course, she crept silently down the side of the outcrop, keeping in its shelter until she arrived within bow shot of her prey.

The warrior was whistling impatiently, trying to rouse a reply from his dead comrade, she thought. As he delivered a last irritated twitter, she shot him neatly through the neck, and he dropped out of sight.

Two. How many would there be? And why were they so cautious about trailing an old woman and three small children?

Despite her haste, she felt driven by that question. She listened hard, heard nothing but the wind, and moved cautiously to the side of this victim. Her arrow had pierced his throat, and his blood still ran sluggishly, but there was no life in him. Yet his face held another wound, this one also fresh.

She turned the head to look more closely. The tiny point of a bird arrow had made that mark, she felt certain. Had her people taken weapons? She tried to remember, but that desperate rush seemed days in the past now. Sohala had carried a supply bundle and Tilepita. The grandmother had been burdened with the healing bag. Had Nitipu or Setichi caught up his small bow as they left the lodge?

Someone had, it was certain, for the distinctive mark of the arrowhead was unmistakable. Ayina smiled grimly. Her people were not fleeing like wounded deer before the hunter. They were evidently pausing from time to time to surprise their pursuers with a small attack—perhaps a trap of the kind that the children used constantly to catch small game.

She recovered her arrow and went forward. Ahead, up the slope and still farther to the southeast, there was a rumble. Ayina was running before she took time to think, heading toward the sound, though she still took care to remain concealed as much as possible.

She had not gone more than a hand of paces when there came a yell of terror—from the throat of a man. The rumble became a grinding roar, and another voice joined the first. Ayina reached high and swung herself into the prickly branches of a juniper tree, where she climbed as high as possible.

What was taking place? Were her people in danger?

When she reached a point from which she could see past the next thicket, she began to smile. The steep slope at that farther part of the ridge was moving, rocks and soil beginning to settle as she had seen happen many times after a rockslide. Far down, almost to the sage and rabbit-brush flats, two distant figures ran desperately to escape the rocks that still bounded after them.

Ayina dropped to the ground and sped up the slope and along the ridge, following it to the top of the slide. As she had suspected, the grandmother stood there, drooping with weariness but still alert, and Sohala and the two remaining small ones were beside her.

"Mother! We pushed the big rock, and it went down *whump*, and everything started to slip after it. One of those men was smashed, and the other two ran very fast! The rocks went after them like coyotes after a rabbit!" the little girl said, all in a rush.

Then she looked past Ayina. "Where is our father?" Her eyes were wide with the beginning of sorrow.

"He will come no more," Ayina said. "He died as a Geh-i-nah, weapon in hand and dead enemies before him. I gave him a secure resting place; we must go on without him."

The grandmother turned to her, her face sorrowful. "Those men shot the small one, and there was no time to care for him. He was dead, and we ran . . . faster than those two down there, I think. Nitipu is gone, Granddaughter."

"I saw," she said. But her heart was filled with a strange triumph. "Yet we have killed some of those who caused his death. You buried one beneath the stones. I killed two back along the ridge. Now we must go again, very fast, for the others may come back and bring still more Tsununni after us."

The grandmother gave a terrible sigh. "I can go no farther, Granddaughter. We stopped to make this trap because my legs will no longer move. Go to your people. Take the children. I will wait here and watch. If they return, I shall take this small bow that Setichi brought and give them something to distract them, while you get far ahead of them."

It was true. Ayina could see in the old woman's eyes that all her strength had been spent. Now her best course was to use what little life she had left to secure the retreat of those of her blood. It was an honorable thing, and Ayina felt quiet pride in this kinswoman of her husband.

"We honor you, Grandmother. Tales will be told around the campfires about the good fight you waged to save your family. I have a bigger bow and two arrows. The small arrows will have more impact from this bow, as well. You will find Tolumme and your grandson in the Other Place. Greet them for me."

She handed the weapon to the old woman and helped her to prop herself up in concealment amid a clump of rocks behind a low-growing juniper. From that spot she would be able to see if Tsununni came to look for footprints where their prey had stopped to cause the slide.

Then she gave the children their burdens again, taking Tilepita upon her own back to save the strength of young Sohala. They raised their hands in farewell, and the grandmother nodded.

Then they turned once more toward the southeast and moved down the other side of the ridge, going as fast as their battered bodies would carry them. If they were not stopped again to do battle, two days and part of another should see them in the stone houses of her kindred.

⇘26↞

The young brides had almost reached their goal. The very same crooked peak that had marked the way to Ayina's marriage clan was in sight, beyond a stretch of rough ridges and sagebrush flats. A handful of days would see the last of the Geh-i-nah at their goal.

But not only the old men were flagging now. Ayina herself, pushed past the limits of her aging body, had slowed, and they camped earlier and rested longer at the end of each day. Ish-o-tobi stayed now by her side, pushing her up steep places or pulling her hands to help.

They were very near her old home now, and she could see the cliffs glowing in the distance as the sun began to descend. "If we should go north and east here, following that river beyond the cliff, we would see what is left of the houses of my clan kin," she said, as Teala helped her onto her bed skins and propped her with a bundle.

She no longer had to be urged to recount the story of that early time. It became clearer to her now than their present as they toiled forward toward their goal.

The others huddled about the fire that Netah kindled in a rocky cup, savoring the warmth, for with night the air became chilly. Old bones needed the comfort of the blaze.

Almost without thinking about her audience, Ayina began to relive the past that had occurred so very near to this camping place.

The welcome, when she and her children came at last to the stone house on the bluff, was kind but distracted. Many others of the western kindred had come near enough to need help, but they had been sent on southward, where there might be more room to house them and more stores to feed them over the winter.

The appearance of so many people, distant kinsmen who had been driven from their homes, robbed of all that made life possible for them, had disturbed Etuni, now very old, and the other elders who watched over the River Geh-i-nah. But when this one who shared their blood came, she was taken in without question. She was their immediate kindred, however crowded the house and its nearby pit houses might be.

Ayina saw very soon that her people dreaded facing the same fate that had overtaken Nosete's people, and she went at last to Etuni and sat before him. "Grandfather, I have seen this enemy. I have killed a hand of the Tsununni, fearsome as they may be. They are not devils risen from the earth or dropped from the sky. They are men, just as we are.

"I will help you to plan, if you wish it, how to deal with them if they come this far."

But the day when Ayina's word as healer bore great

weight had passed. Now she was a widow with small
children, and though she again lent a hand to Ketala,
her old apprentice, the people had lost their trust in
her. She had been gone too long.

"We who are old will deal with the Tsununni. Tend
your children, Ayina, and let us manage," he told
her.

For a long while she did just that, gathering foodstuffs from the mountain and the river, working skins,
making ointments of herbs and tallow or teas to help
the sick. The winter, when it came, was harsh, and
the stores were barely sufficient to keep the clan until
spring. When the snow melted and ran away down
the mountain to turn the gullies below into rushing
torrents, many had sores on their skins or loose teeth
in their skulls.

Ayina dosed and massaged and tended everyone,
but when Sohala fell ill she felt her heart grow cold.
The child's warm brown face held a bluish tint, and
her cough grew deeper and deeper, despite steam
baths and stronger and stronger doses of herbal infusions.

Her sister knew, before Ayina would admit it, that
the child was dead. Then the grieving mother sat
for a long time holding the lax hand, touching the
silky hair, knowing that her daughter was past help
or pain.

Both her sisters understood her grief, for everyone
lost children, and they had counted their own dead.
They took Setichi and Tilepita among their own young
ones and diverted their childish grief with tales and
games.

At last, Tanat came to Ayina, who was sitting on a rock pounding moss for poultices. "You work too hard, and you think too much," she said, touching her shoulder.

"Always you were successful at finding new plants and new places. Why do you not go down again into the lowlands and search for herbs, as you used to do? Spring has melted the snows, and water is everywhere. It would, I think, be a good thing for you to do."

Ayina stared out across the wooded canyon below her perch. With sudden shock, she realized that she had no real responsibilities. No husband, no child, now that her last two were gathered into her sisters' families, no parent left to tend. She was free to go where she pleased, but the thought was not pleasure but acute pain.

Yet she knew that she must do something, or else she might be tempted to cast herself over the cliff and end her life on the stones below. To be useless was a thing she had never felt before. She seemed unable to deal with the idea.

"I will go, my sister. Thank you for being my eyes and my mind, for I have been lost in a bitter dream this past winter. I will go right now to tell Etuni and the elders, for they may have some errand I might do for them in the lowlands."

But the elders still had no use for this returned member of their clan, and when she went it was with no set goal in her mind. However, when she reached the gullied land where the snowmelt cut the country into rough canyons, she had a sudden thought.

There would be no concern if she was gone for many

hands of days—or, she suspected, forever. Why should she not go north to that great cliff from which the Ahye-tum-datsehe had come? Those people seemed to have managed to keep the Tsununni at bay, and it was in her mind to find Ku-la-ti, if he had managed to return from his exile, and his companion, whose name she did not know.

The description they had given of their houses in the cliffs still puzzled her. Perhaps there might be a way that her own people could use the cliff along their river as protection.

So she turned her steps to the north, following streams as much as possible, crossing wide stretches of sagebrush and odd round stones like those beneath the river. Her gourds of water were heavy, but she did not trust that she might always find streams when they were needed. She struggled beneath their weight, as well as that of her basket and the plants she had gathered.

The way was very long, and never did she see that arrogant cliff, though she followed the sequence of rivers, just as Ku-la-ti had described them to her. Landmark followed landmark, and at last she came over a great shoulder of land and saw on the edge of the world the shape she remembered.

It was even bigger than she had thought, for no scribble in the dust can ever represent the great being that is a mountain. It rose above shaggy forest, thrusting its head into a drift of cloud. She had never been so high, she thought, and if she climbed it—excitement stirred her heart—she could see forever over the country beyond it.

She knew that the Ahye-tum-datsehe kept close

watch on the lands below their mesa, so she stopped, once she was within a slow day's journey of her goal, and built a signal fire. Its column of smoke rose straight, sheltered from the wind by the bulk of the mesa itself, and she knew that someone above would see it. If she were fortunate, someone would also come to see who had entered their lands.

Settling herself beside the blaze, she waited patiently for some reply. In this time of danger, surely people who meant each other no harm might band together to protect themselves from enemies.

She chewed some dried meat, drank water from a gourd, and waited still. Night came, and she left the fire to climb into a cluster of boulders. Predators were always a danger, and she had no wish to end in the belly of a puma.

With the dawn, she woke to the sound of a hesitant birdcall. Not one of the raucous jays, though it sounded like it. No, that call came from the lips of a man, and she rose among her nest of boulders and whistled shrilly.

Then, carrying no weapon, she went down to the remnant of the fire, whose smoke still wisped upward from the burned-out coals. Beside it stood three wiry men, much like the three she had met back along her own river when she was a girl.

She pointed toward them. "Ahye-tum-datsehe?" she asked.

They stared at her sharply, then turned to confer among themselves. The oldest stepped forward at last and nodded.

She thought back to that old meeting. "*E'ht Geh-i-nah*," she said. "*Ayina*." She pointed to herself. Then, hopefully, she asked, "Ihyati? Ku-la-ti?"

The old man's eyes narrowed, and he nodded once, decisively. Turning, he gestured for her to follow, and the four of them went down and up and across wooded country, moving at speed. Even though she was weary from her journey, Ayina made no complaint and did not slow the pace.

When they came at last to the great mesa, which now towered over them as if to fall and crush them beneath its bulk, she was stunned by its size. The morning sun had lit it to gold as they approached it. Now the afternoon sun was reddening the visible side as they scrambled upward through small oaks and up steep rocks.

When at last they emerged onto the top, the sun was halved on the horizon, and the land below lay rimmed with shadows. She had never seen anything like it; she paused involuntarily. The old man turned to see what she found so interesting, and for a moment he, too, stared out over the country below the mesa. His expression softened slightly, as if he shared her delight in the vista lying beneath his home.

Then they turned again toward his destination. Ayina went forward, hoping that one of the men she had met in her life would still be living among these stranger people.

⤢27⤡

"That was perhaps the strangest time of my whole life," the old woman said to her clustered listeners. "It was like visiting the Other Place, very near the sky, with plants and creatures that were like and yet different from those I knew.

"The people themselves were wary of me, at first, until Ku-la-ti returned from a visit to kin on the other side of the mesa. He recognized me at once, and we managed to draw pictures and make sign until he told me the story of his journey home, after the Tsununni passed through the country and disappeared."

"You mean they just went away?" asked Teala.

"Indeed, no," said Ayina. "But the Tsununni, even to this day, come when no one expects them and go when they have done what they intended. No man can say what they want, other than food stores and such things, and I have wondered if they have not been driven as our own people were, time after time, by enemies or by problems they could not control or understand."

She touched Ish-o-tobi's shoulder lightly. "However it was, they passed through and were gone, and he found his way home again. He told his people of the help our village gave him, and he told them my name. That is why the men who came to meet me brought me onto the mesa, for otherwise they would have driven me away or killed me. The Tsununni make every kind of people very cautious with strangers."

Once Ku-la-ti had identified her as the very woman he had known, it seemed that the Ahye-tum-datsehe relaxed, feeling that she was, in some way, one of their own. In a very short time, surrounded by their talk all day, Ayina was able to understand their words and to speak in her turn.

There was one man, very old, very wise, called the One Who Smelled the Wind. He, in particular, liked to sit beside her on the cliff, watching the land below, raising his head from time to time to sniff the air, as if for danger or change.

It was he who told her much of the history of this mesa-top kind. In so doing he spoke often of his predecessor Uhtatse, in the the past, who had caused his people to move down into the cliffsides.

Ayina found that extremely interesting. "My own people live on the edge of a cliff, though not one so high or so steep as this. Yet it might be that they could go down, dig homes into the sides as you have done, and so hold off the Tsununni if they come so far."

The old man shook his head. "Unless your cliff has natural caves worn back into the rock, it would take more lifetimes than any people can expect to do the work. Unless the cliff below is so steep that a child with rocks can hold off an attacking horde, the work itself would be useless."

So, then, Ayina thought, her journey had been hopeless. And yet, there on that high mesa, she did find useful plants that did not grow in the place where she lived. There were old women who had tried healing techniques unknown among her own people and who used common plants in unusual ways. In her turn, she told them of matters that old Susuni had taught her as a child and that she had devised for herself.

When the time came to leave at last, she felt she was going away from kinsfolk, not strangers. Ku-la-ti, in particular, seemed saddened to see her go.

As she stood at the top of the steep climb down to the Middle Way, he was there with his family and the old One Who Smelled the Wind.

"Sister," he said to her, "let us not lose this newly woven tie between our people. In the summer we send hunters south into the lower country. When the Twin Rabbits hang just above the eastern horizon at sunset, that is when we go. If you will build a signal fire near the crooked peak you showed us when we were with your people, there will be a sharing of news and a trading of goods between us."

The old shaman nodded. "We learned in the time of Uhtatse that new things can be very good. Let us not lose this chance at learning new skills and ways. If only with warnings of danger, we may be of benefit to each other."

Then she went down the difficult way and turned her steps again to the south and the east, working her way through the maze of canyons and mesas toward her home once again. And this time when she arrived she brought word that interested Etuni and the other elders, though still they would not listen to her warnings about the Tsununni.

The years passed quickly, as they tend to do when one is busy with work and children and the many responsibilities of keeping people fed and clothed, healthy and trained to do the thousand tasks of living. Ayina's surviving children grew tall; suddenly little Tilepita was glancing shyly sideways at a young man from one of the pit houses along the cliff.

Setichi was not long in following his sister into marriage with a young woman from the third stone house built over the upper part of the river. Ayina found herself a grandmother twice over within the space of a single year.

The two granddaughters were her joy and her wonder, for both had a look of Nosete, at least to her eyes. She tended them and taught them, and both, from the time they were toddlers, learned so quickly that she knew they had something of her ability. By the time they were as tall as her waist, they promised to become healers to rival even her old teacher Susuni.

Every year, the signal fire was lit by runners sent to the crooked peak, and usually Ayina went with them to greet her old friends from the high mesa. Sometimes they told of attacks by the Tsununni, but even those determined people had all but given up trying to conquer the people who lived in the cliffs.

Sometimes they spoke of the weather, which was by turns too bitterly cold and too dry. Always they renewed friendship between the two peoples and kept abreast of the families of Ayina and Ku-la-ti. This became so much a tradition that no one ever considered neglecting the demanding journey to the crooked peak when the time of meeting came.

The granddaughters grew, Susa becoming tall and slender, Nepe smaller and more fragile. Ayina took great pride in them, and Setichi and Tilepita left them more and more to their grandmother's care as they attended to other tasks and younger children. The girls revered her and seemed destined to become great healers, in their own rights.

Yet when the time for the signal fire came, they remained at home and Ayina went with the runners toward the peak where the signal must be set. For the first time no Ahye-tum-datsehe waited there, and when the third day came and went, the four other messengers, though they were all older than she, looked to Ayina for guidance.

"If they have not come, there is some real and dreadful reason for it. Let us run home as fast as we may, for I have a bad feeling in my heart. If the Tsununni . . ." But she could not finish that sentence.

They ran, indeed, and though Ayina was already nearing middle age, she forced her legs to match strides with those of the hard-muscled men who accompanied her. Fear filled them all as they went, and she could feel it in her companions, reinforcing the chill that clenched about her heart.

They approached the long ridge with its great peak rearing above the forested slopes, and there they slowed, keeping to ravines or clumps of sagebrush. If their fears were well founded, there might be watchers who were no friends of theirs.

As they came to the trees, they spread out for concealment, each finding his own way up the steep, hidden to some extent by the thick tree trunks, clumps of young spruce, and the pitch of the ground itself. Ayina followed a route she knew well.

Farther up, she had climbed that exact tree as a child to escape the grizzly. Beyond, where the shoulder of the mountain rounded a bit and eased the slope, she had picked mullein leaves. That winter the smoke from those dried leaves had eased the cough of her own mother.

Though the memories flooded her mind, her senses remained alert; by the time she came over the top of the ridge and started down the other side she smelled smoke. Not that of cook fires. Not that of any normal daily activity.

This smoke was tinged with something terrible and sickening. A wail rose in her throat, but never in all her life had Ayina lost control of herself, and she did not now. The footpath worn by the children as they gathered wood from the forest and brought it back down to the cliffside houses beckoned to her, but she did not take that easier way. If enemies were below, they would watch the paths.

The better course for her would be to run fast and far, never looking back, but that was impossible to one of her people. She must know what had happened to her family and her clan, whatever suffering it might cause her.

As she went down toward the river cliffs, Ayina lay flat and slithered along like a snake, keeping in the deepest shadow of the huge conifers. Once she spotted a rattlesnake ahead, sunning himself on a rock that

caught a stray beam of sunlight trickling through the
high branches, but she circled wide, and the creature
never knew she was near.

She had learned in the school of survival the ways to
conceal her presence. When she came to a point from
which she could see the stone house where she had
been born, not even the gray bird sitting in the tangled
twigs above her gave any hint of her presence.

Peering out from a patch of rough grass, her face
concealed by stalks of young mullein, Ayina saw the
smoke rising from the structure below her. Even as
she watched, a hand of Tsununni came into view,
circling, bows ready to pick off any survivor of the
blaze who might try to escape from his burning home.

A child's shriek came clearly to the healer's ears,
and she had to hold on to the earth beneath her hands
to keep from running forward to help. Her death, she
knew too well, would not aid any of her family, who
now were dead or dying. Yet she must watch this to
the end. Something inside her demanded that.

If she saw the Tsununni at this work, that vision,
added to the death of Nosete's village, would make
her careful, devious, secretive, for the rest of her life.
If any people at all survived from this disaster, she
would find them and take them far away. She would
make certain they never found themselves in this terrible predicament again.

The dry pine stringers crackled loudly, and from
time to time the stones themselves exploded. The
enemy warriors backed away as the fire grew hot-
ter and no more cries came from the fiery ruin.
Ayina watched closely as the men turned at last to
go. . . .

Downriver, toward the next stone house. Had the other four already been destroyed? Her heart felt sodden in her chest, but she did not allow her grief to affect her actions. Sliding through the forest that she knew so well, she kept the men in sight as they went.

She would, if nothing else, find a way to kill at least one of them before she was done. But as she moved around a thicket of young spruce she caught a tiny sound. A smothered gasp?

Lying on her belly, she crept into the edge of the thicket and hissed. Then, in the softest whisper she could manage, she said, "It is Ayina. Are any of my people here?"

There was a moment of dead silence, unbroken even by the light breeze through the spruce. Then, "Ayina. It is good. I have brought the children. Now I die, and you must take them from my hands."

She squirmed forward into the prickly branches, broke free into a tiny opening, and saw three very small girls huddled together, eyes wide, beside a hunched shape.

"Tanat?" she asked.

It was her sister, her leather skirt bloody, her bare shoulders streaked with ash and blood. The eyes that looked up at her were already dulling, but Tanat's will held her there to speak again.

"My daughters are dead. Your children and grand-children are, also. But I have saved three who will carry forward our blood. Teala, Netah, Pulap will be your grandchildren now, my sister. Farewell."

The eyes closed, and Tanat was no longer there. Ayina looked into the frightened faces of the little girls and sighed. They must not be risked, and yet she could not leave her sister's bones to predators. The fact that she had been forced to leave her small son untended, so many seasons in the past, still troubled her heart. She must not do that again.

"Dig," she whispered to the small ones.

Obediently, they began scrabbling in the loose scurf of soil and needles under the trees, and soon the four of them had scraped out a shallow cup whose bottom was the pale stone of the mountain. Then Ayina pulled her sister's body into the grave, straightened her limbs, and covered her with all the soil they had moved, as well as any loose slabs of bark or stone she could find among the spruces.

She listened hard, but there was no sound now, not even the popping of the ruins. The Tsununni had gone forward, but she could no longer stalk them. She must make certain that these small ones survived.

Bending her face close to theirs, she spoke softly. "There are four men who came with me from the west. We must wait for them. The enemy will soon go, for that is their way, and then Sekto, Abani, Eketan, and Pahket will come looking for me."

There was no better place she could think of to hide than this, so the healer gathered the small ones about her, comforting their shaking with hugs and pats until they fell asleep from exhaustion. Then she sat, alert as any squirrel on a branch or hawk in the sky, listening for a signal that those men who had gone with her to set the signal fire had come at last to find her.

⤝28⤜

The child in Ayina's lap squirmed to look up at her. "And they came," he said, as if reassuring himself that it had indeed happened so. "And there they sit, all four."

"Yes, they came. We hid and we ran by turns until we won clear of the mountains. Then we followed streams that by then were all but dry. We darted from clump to clump of brush to conceal ourselves from any who might spy us from the heights that surrounded us. We came through the mountains and deserts that the nine of us have just crossed again; in the end we arrived at the place where we built our lodges."

She sighed, thinking of those lost days, the terror and despair that had haunted her dreams for many seasons. She could still hear, if she allowed herself, the child's scream from the burning house. It had been her conviction that it was one of her granddaughters who cried out to her for help that she had been unable to give.

Sekto cleared his throat and spat. "It was a long journey, and we all were glad of its end. The mountain we found seemed to have no dwellers so high, except for the beasts and the birds. We knew that we must keep quiet and take no risks, for there was no way to know where the Tsununni might travel next, so we learned caution."

He peered sideways at Ayina. "It may be that otherwise we would have waited too long and allowed those who hunted the boy to come upon us. Only through surprise might a small band like this, mostly those who are too old or inexperienced for close work with spear and knife, manage to overcome fit warriors."

Teala leaned forward to put a bit of wood on the small fire. "How did you find the Ahye-tum-datsehe again? I know that the young men came to our mountain, but never have you told us how they knew where to find us."

Ayina patted Ish-o-tobi absently. "That was not an accident. Do you recall the summer when you were as high as my shoulder, Granddaughter?"

The girl looked at her sharply. "That was the year when you left us for many hands of days. Indeed, when you returned it was fall again, and we had barely managed to do all the tasks you left for us while you were gone."

The healer nodded. "I knew from the beginning that something must be done to secure the future for my granddaughters. You were three, all growing skillful at the healing arts, which are all I had to teach you. It would be sad if your lives were wasted in tending us until we died and then in wearing out your own existences on that cold mountain.

"As soon as you were old enough to do the work under the care of the men, I knew that I must go back to the crooked mountain and build the signal fire. If any of the Ahye-tum-datsehe remained, surely they would still send hunters on their yearly journey. It was the only way I knew to find some life for you after I am gone."

Eketan shifted his aching legs and pushed one of the dogs aside. "We knew what she was trying, and we thought her mad. A woman alone, crossing this difficult country, could hardly accomplish what she attempted. Yet we agreed that you children were the most important of us all. We must remain behind to protect you. It was a long wait, and we grew fearful, as the days grew shorter and the wind chilled with early storms."

The journey had been more difficult than before, for Ayina was older, wearier. She was not driven by fear of the Tsununni, and she did not have the children to hurry to some place of safety. Only her will pushed her over the ridges, through the dry flatlands, up and down the ravines.

When at last she came within sight of the crooked peak, tears leaked from her eyes, for she remembered her first sight of it. Nosete had been beside her, and their life together had just begun. As she took the way she remembered, she could almost feel her husband at her elbow, helping her along this last, most difficult stretch of her journey.

Indeed, she almost turned to speak to him, but something warned her that this might take away that warm presence. So she forged ahead, until she reached the old spot where signal fires had been lit over many summers.

The rocky cup was still marked with soot from those earlier fires, and she gathered brush and bits of dead juniper and pine and arranged her fire. She piled extra fuel nearby, located a sleeping place out of sight but near enough to watch and listen, and kindled her signal blaze.

Then, fearful that some enemy might also be attracted to the column of smoke, she hid, high among the boulders, and lay resting, waiting for some sign that her message might be seen. She drifted into and out of sleep, but some part of her awareness was always on duty.

The day passed, and she covered the fire, for those she sought would not travel in darkness. The next morning she fed the remaining coals and brought the fire to life again. For a hand of days she kept her watch, gathering more wood, looking afar from the top of a nearby cliff, wondering more and more if she had wasted her efforts.

She had found a nearby ridge that was not so difficult that she risked injury in climbing it. Every morning, after making the fire, she went up and lay flat on the warm rock at the top, shaded by a skimpy juniper. She could see over a wide stretch of land, making out even deer and elk as they browsed on the rabbit brush and scrub.

There was no sign that anyone hunted here now. She felt that all her people had fled or died; any who remained must be lost remnants like her own, hiding in small groups in remote places. The thought saddened her, as she recalled the days when many people hunted or gathered seeds and herbs in the lands that now lay empty.

As she mused, her alert gaze caught a hint of motion far at the edge of the scrubland. A mule deer bounded into sight and out again as it dived into some hidden ravine. Ayina pushed herself up with both hands, keeping herself hidden in the juniper branches but watching closely. After a moment, she saw a tiny shape trot across a barren space and disappear into the rocks beyond it.

Someone was coming. She crept down the cliff and fed the fire again, making certain that the column of smoke rose dark into the burning sky. Then she hid again and kept watch.

They came cautiously, which told her that they, too, had known the attentions of enemies. One climbed to a high spot and stared down into the cupped place where the fire burned. Then he was gone, and still she waited.

At last she could see the men who were approaching, and her heart leaped with joy. They wore the simple garments and carried the beautifully woven gathering bags that she remembered from her visit to the Ahye-tum-datsehe. Their faces held the stamp of that people, she found as she stared toward the approaching hunters.

"Greeting, friends. Is the name Ayina remembered among your people?" she called in their own tongue, though she did not yet reveal herself.

A deep voice boomed in echoes from the cliffs. "The Ahye-tum-datsehe have long wondered about their friend Ayina and her people. Ku-la-ti, her particular friend, spoke of her before he died two winters past."

Reassured, she stood and began making her way down the rocky slope on which she had concealed herself. The men below had their weapons in hand, but she did not blame them for that. It was only good sense to make certain before taking any risk.

When she stood beside the band of hunters, she recognized two of them as men who had been boys when she visited the great mesa. "E-pi-tat!" she said, smiling at the first. "And Ko-le-nek! You were children when last I saw you."

It was a good time; once meat was sputtering over the fire, the group sat about, exchanging news of old friends. Ayina learned that others besides Ku-la-ti had died since her last contact with the roving hunters.

"The Tsununni came," E-pi-tat said, when she asked about that dreadful summer when the signal fire brought no reply. "They ranged below the mesa, and we spared no man to hunt that season, for we expected them to attack us at any time. Yet they did not; they hunted the lands about the foot of our mesa, and at last they moved away toward the south."

"Ah," she sighed. "They would be the ones that destroyed my people's houses and drove us far away. My own family died. I fled, taking with me those who had come to the crooked peak with me and three small girls. We have lived far to the east, since that time."

The men urged her to tell of that last attack on her people, and again she lived that terrible time, seeing the fire wrap the stone house, hearing the cry of the child inside. The men shuddered as she spoke, and

when she fell silent at last they sat quiet, thinking of
what they had heard.

"My people did not expect to be attacked, even
after my other village was destroyed," she told them.
"They took no extra precautions, though I urged them
to travel to your mesa and ask for advice on dealing
with the Tsununni. You are the only people I know
who seem to be safe from their attacks."

"The gods gave us our mesa, with its caves in the
cliffs. Otherwise we might have been driven away, as
your Geh-i-nah were," said Uh-la-gi, the eldest of the
men. "It is only when we speak with others that we
understand how fortunate we are. But we wonder . . .
why have you made the journey again to the crooked
peak? It is too far and too hard to attempt for any
unimportant reason."

She nodded. "I have given thought to the future,"
she said. "Of all the Geh-i-nah, the only survivors I
know are four men who even now are well into old
age and three young girls. In time they will need husbands and a village to give them protection. When
they are grown, they will be alone, for the men and
I will not live forever."

"It is a difficult problem," Uh-la-gi said. He didn't
sound as if he intended to offer a solution, but Ayina
had not expected for her task to be an easy one.

"I am training my granddaughters as healers," she
said. "It is my way, and I was trained by the greatest
healer our people knew. All three of the girls, young
as they are, have become skilled, and one of them has
a great gift for the art.

"No people ever have too many healers, and I
remember the great numbers of clans living on your

mesa. So many people need midwives, those who can cure cuts and bruises, coughing sickness and all the other ills that every people suffer."

The men sat for a long time, as if thinking. Then Uh-la-gi said, "You have good words. If the children grow to adulthood, and if they are all sound healers, it may be that there will be those among our clans who will ask for them as brides. But how will we know when the time comes?"

Ayina leaned forward, her heart burning with purpose. "In five summers, the three will be of marriage-able age. If you will find three young men who will offer them their protection, then have them come to our mountain at that time.

"I will tell you how to find it so they will have no trouble reaching us. If they find my granddaughters acceptable, and if the girls are drawn to them, we will make a marriage promise. Then, at an agreed time, we will come here to this spot under the crooked peak and meet the bridegrooms and their families.

"Go back to the mesa, when your hunt is over, and ask among your kind. I think you will find those who will welcome the granddaughters of Ayina the healer."

"And that is how the three young men knew how to find our mountain!" said Netah, her eyes wide. "I never asked Tu-a-lim, when we were talking together. It seemed that some magic had sent the young men to us."

"Uh-la-gi and I talked and drew lines in the dirt until he knew how to direct them. And now we are here under the peak at the appointed time. If nothing terrible has happened to the Ahye-tum-datsehe, they will come soon." She nodded across the fire at her granddaughters, who sat shoulder to shoulder, their faces warmed with the red light.

They were comely women, she knew, skilled and brave. This last trial had tempered them, made them even stronger than before. The families on the mesa were getting good wives for their sons.

ᕗ29ᕐ

It was several days before the bridegrooms came, attended by the new One Who Smelled the Wind, the old healer that Ayina remembered from her visit to the mesa, and numbers of relatives from all three clans involved. The travelers seemed easy and free of any fear of enemies, for the Tsununni, it seemed, had struck the summer before. Never did the fierce people come twice together, now.

Ayina greeted those she knew with joy, for they, too, had grown old. There would be no other meeting, she felt certain, even with her granddaughters. Her heart felt both sore and strangely free, as if she had been loosed from a heavy burden.

She watched the wedding chant, the dance of the few young women who had come with the Ahye-tum-datsehe, the wrapping of the robe about the three couples. Her granddaughters were safe, with the possibility of long and useful lives before them. The old men were more than capable of caring for themselves; they had proved that as they traveled over the terrible country behind them.

She embraced the young women and politely avoided the eyes of their husbands. She celebrated with the older people through the days until it was time for them to turn their steps homeward. But all the while she felt strangely light in the bone, as if she might be able to float like dust on the wind.

She watched her granddaughters and their new families growing smaller and smaller as they moved away down the country below her high perch. Ish-o-tobi, smaller than any, was not to be seen among the taller people around him. The sun was in the east, lighting the faces of the cliffs in the west, and in that warm dazzle the distant figures seemed magical, as if they went away into the Other Place instead of toward the great mesa.

Then they were gone from sight. The old men, sitting beside the dead fire, spoke softly, but Ayina sat alone beneath a pine, watching the sky grow brighter, the sun shimmer on rocks and bushes and slide in layers of light and cloud shadow across the country beneath her.

She was alone at last, except for the four old men, here within a hand of days travel from the last home of her people.

The wind sang through pine and juniper, magpies squawked overhead, chipmunks scampered, and eagles soared so high in the vault of the sky that their screeches were almost inaudible. There was no sound of any human voice, no shout of returning hunters or laughter of playing children. Never again would there be unless some other people, younger and newly come to this country, made their home here.

Ayina smiled. She had no pregnant women to tend. There would be no wounds to clean and dress or limbs to remove with her flint and obsidian knives and axes and notched saws.

She would forget the smell of blood, in time; the groans of women in labor or men in the throes of death would fade from her ears. Perhaps the song of wind and the rush of leaves would replace the cries of pain that had surrounded her for so much of her adult life.

A chipmunk skittered across the ledge of rock at her feet, its round cheeks stuffed with piñon nuts or grass seeds. It paused for a moment to dart a bright glance at her, deciding if she posed a threat.

With only herself and the old men, now, she needed no meat for the pot. They ate, the lot of them, so little that a child could have fed the entire group and been left with time for play. No, she needed no tiny scrap of meat like the chipmunk, so for the first time she remained still and watched as the small creature darted to the shelter of a rock, looked about, darted again, and gained the safety of the clump of bushes toward which he was heading.

She realized that she had never really *watched* an animal before. Not just for the pleasure of learning how it moved and what it might be thinking. Animals had meant principally either meat or danger.

She had observed intently as she hunted beasts: deer and marmoset, rabbits and even elk. What she hunted, she usually brought down. Even now, her bones aching and her eyesight dimmed, she would have no trouble in providing for herself. But it seemed better, she found, to watch than to kill.

Sheer pleasure warmed her old bones as she waited for the chipmunk to return. This she could do simply for herself, enjoying her respite from responsibilities and dangers.

If an enemy came, one of the Tsununni, perhaps, and slew her as she sat here, it would be no loss. The old men were fully capable of caring for themselves. Her granddaughters were gone to a new people, where their healing skills would bring them honor. Ish-o-tobi had been welcomed warmly by his new people, for children were always valuable.

The summer was full blown. Suddenly, her bones longed to move across the country once more toward the last home of her people, the stone houses that the Tsununni had burned. Perhaps if she stood once more at the place where her people had died, it might ease the child's cry that still haunted her dreams.

Were the ruins of the stone houses of the Geh-i-nah still standing on the promontories along the river? Burned though they might be, the stones should stand long after her own bones were dust, for they were massive and well cut, fitted together solidly.

She longed to walk even farther, if she still had the strength after reaching that first goal. She would like to go where her mother's mothers had passed, east and south, east and north to the lands whose descriptions she had stored in her memory along with the history of the Geh-i-nah.

The aches in her bones might not allow that, she understood. The dimness of her eyes would get worse, with time. Now, while she was fit from this last long effort, still able to see clearly enough to avoid danger, was the time to make this final journey.

Ayina, the healer of the Geh-i-nah, stood decisively, and the chipmunk, just venturing on another trip to his source of seeds, leaped back into the shelter of the rocks. The magpies perched above her head gave raucous cries and flapped up in a flurry of black and white.

As if noticing even such a small movement below him, the eagle tilted a wing and drifted lazily downward on the wind, passing close above her as she stood at the edge of the cliff, staring eastward, now, instead of toward the north, where her granddaughters had gone to their new families. Its long cry echoed among the mountains and in Ayina's heart.

She had no wings, like the eagle or the magpies. She was not young and spry, like the chipmunk. But she had feet that still walked, legs that could carry her worn body a long way still, before they failed.

She could find food where many would starve, and she could tend her own illnesses with herbal concoctions.

Ayina turned, her leather skirt whispering against the pine, and moved toward the ashes of the wedding fire. She would say good-bye to Sekto and Eketan, to Pahket and Abani. They might live here, where there was water nearby and game that few hunted. It would be good for them to be active instead of sinking again into the laziness of their time on that distant mountainside.

Now Ayina would live beneath the sky, and only when winter came would she worry about freezing. There was a considerable distance before her feet, and if she lived to reach her goal and stand beside the ashes of her children, she would be satisfied. If she went even farther, it would be a great gift from the gods, who now seemed more credible and much nearer than they had when she was young.

Winter would not be a problem, she felt in her heart. She might well die as so many of her kind had done on the harsh journey they had made in the distant past. But she would see with her own eyes, rather than those of her memory, the places of which she had spoken to the granddaughters.

While the old men sat talking over the great days when they were young, Ayina gathered her bundle of tools and weapons, rolled up her stout deer hide, and set fresh coals in the clay-lined gourd.

They were not surprised when she stopped to bid them good-bye. She could see in their eyes that they were preparing themselves for the Other Place, even as she was.

Setting her gaze on the distant peak toward the east, she began her journey into the past. The child's cry was fading in her memory, even as she went into the rough country that lay between the crooked peak and the great ridge that lay above the river of her people. Her feet moved quickly, and the ache in her bones was less than it had been for a very long while.

Ayina, healer of the Geh-i-nah, was going home again.

FREE
Romance
(a $4.50 value)

Send in the Coupon Below

To get your FREE historical
romance and start saving, fill out
the coupon below and mail it today.
As soon as we receive it we'll send
you your FREE Book along with
your first month's selections.
